Point of Ignition

Acclaim for Erin Dutton's Fiction

"*Sequestered Hearts* by first time novelist, Erin Dutton, is everything a romance should be. It is teeming with longing, heartbreak, and of course, love…as pure romances go, it is one of the best in print today." —*Just About Write*

"*Fully Involved* starts with a bang as fire engines race toward a fire at the downtown Hilton Hotel…Dutton literally fills the pages with smoke as she vividly describes the scene. She is equally skilled at showing her readers Reid's feelings of guilt and rage…*Fully Involved* explores the emotional depths of…two very different women. Each woman struggles with loss, change, and the magnetic attraction they have for each other. Their relationship sizzles, flames, and ignites with a page turning intensity. This is an exciting read about two very intriguing women." —*Just About Write*

"Back when Isabel Grant was the tag-along little sister who annoyed them, tomboy Reid Webb and boyhood pal Jimmy Grant considered the girl an intrusion…Years later, Isabel…comes back into Reid's life… and childhood frictions—complicated by Reid's guilty attraction to Isabel—flare into emotional warfare. This being a lesbian romance, no plot points are spoiled by the fact that Reid and Isabel, both stubborn to the core, end up in each other's arms. But Dutton's studied evocation of the macho world of firefighting gives the formulaic story extra oomph—and happily ever after is what a good romance is all about, right?" —*Q Syndicate*

"*Designed for Love* is …rich in love, romance, and sex. Dutton gives her readers a roller coaster ride filled with sexual thrills and chills as Jillian and Wil battle the attraction between them. *Designed for Love* is the perfect book to curl up with on a cold winter's day." —*Just About Write*

By the Author

Sequestered Hearts

Fully Involved

A Place to Rest

Designed for Love

Point of Ignition

Point of Ignition

by

Erin Dutton

2009

POINT OF IGNITION

ISBN 10: 1-60282-084-8
ISBN 13: 978-1-60282-084-5

This Trade Paperback Original Is Published By
Bold Strokes Books, Inc.
P.O. Box 249
Valley Falls, NY 12185

First Edition: July 2009

Credits
Editor: Shelley Thrasher
Production Design: Stacia Seaman
Cover Design By Sheri (graphicartist2020@hotmail.com)

Acknowledgments

If there is one thing I learned while I was writing this book, it's that life goes on…whether you're prepared for it or not. And that the most wonderful things can happen even when you refuse to plan. And that there will always be times when I'm stressed, or worried, or wishing I had more hours in the day. But life is about grabbing every moment of happiness, cherishing the love, and breathing as much fresh air as I can on those perfect, warm, and clear summer days.

That said, I need to thank Shelley for your patience during this process. In the end, I'm so proud of what we did.

Radclyffe, I'm so grateful for the faith you continue to put in my work. I can't believe this makes number five. It seems like only yesterday we were discussing a contract for the first one. It's been an amazing ride and I could not ask for a better guide.

Jennifer Knight, Senior Editor Extraordinaire, thank you for a much needed heart-to-heart phone call. And for not choosing me to act in the skit in Palm Springs. Just kidding. Sort of.

Sheri, you've given me another awesome cover. I bow in homage to your talent.

Dedication

For Christina
you renew my faith in romance every day.

CHAPTER ONE

I need two apple martinis, a screwdriver, and a Long Island iced tea."

"Three Heinekens, a mudslide, two cosmos, and a vodka, neat."

Alexi Clark acknowledged each server with a quick nod, already pouring liquor with both hands. She'd been tending bar for more than half her thirty-nine years and could fill even the most complex orders with ease. But these days, as part owner in this particular bar, she spent less time slinging drinks and more time hunched over a desk in the office. So she actually enjoyed the nights when she could get behind the bar.

The hectic pace of the typical Friday night made time pass quickly. And though she knew she would be worn out by the time the shift was over, she took a measure of pride in the people filling every table and sitting elbow to elbow at the bar. During peak tourist season, they drew a good share of out-of-towners. But her core customer base consisted of local sports fans, many of them regulars.

Alexi credited her staff with much of their success. Her bartenders were knowledgeable and able to suggest the perfect drink for any occasion. She'd relented when her business partner insisted that the servers be mostly women, young and attractive. But she made sure they understood that while friendliness was perfectly acceptable, they were to remain professional as well. And Alexi had won the argument over uniforms, nixing the too-short shorts in favor of khakis and polos. She wouldn't let her establishment have the same reputation as a certain wing joint just a few blocks away.

"Two Budweiser drafts and two Lights in a bottle," one of Alexi's most dependable waitresses called as she passed a food order through the window to the kitchen.

Alexi tilted a mug under the tap and pulled the lever.

"You still here?" Alexi's business partner, Ron Volk, asked as he moved behind the bar. He uncapped two beers and set them on a tray next to her drinks. A nasty flu had been making the rounds of their employees, and tonight, two of their bartenders were among the casualties. Ron and Alexi had taken up the slack, and now it was only three hours until closing time.

Alexi laughed and draped an arm over his shoulders. He was built like a bulldog, short in stature but broad and muscled through his chest and shoulders. "This place is my life. You, on the other hand, have a beautiful wife waiting at home. So get out of here. I'll close."

"You sure?" He pushed his wire-rimmed glasses up his nose in what Alexi was sure was a habit he didn't even notice.

"Yes."

Ron's wife, Danielle, had been Alexi's friend since their early twenties when they tended bar together in a dive on Woodland Street. Of course, that had been before East Nashville became the trendy young-professional-and-coffee-shop area it was now.

"She's probably asleep already."

"Go. I've got this." Alexi took the towel he twisted in his hands and draped it over her shoulder. She pulled a bottle of vodka and flipped it in the air, then caught it and filled the glass in front of her.

"Circus tricks don't impress me," Ron said dryly.

"Get out of my bar." Alexi grinned and slid the drink across the polished mahogany bar she'd restored herself seven years before when she and Ron bought the dilapidated building downtown. Situated one block off Broadway, the building's location was good enough to justify the months of work it had taken to get the place in shape before opening.

Ron waved as he headed for the kitchen and the back door beyond. Alexi grinned and went back to filling drink orders. Cheers from patrons who watched the highlights from that night's hockey game punctuated the steady hum of conversation in the room. Rumor had it that the Predators had a shot at the Stanley Cup this year, and Nashvillians were really getting behind the team. Alexi still wasn't convinced that the perpetually unreliable team could pull it off, but if they did, it would be good for business. She had carefully positioned eight flat-screen televisions around the room so customers could see one from anywhere, and they were usually tuned to a variety of sporting events.

Hours later, as Alexi retrieved the remote from behind the bar and turned off each television, she made mental notes on some promotions the bar could offer if the Preds got into the playoffs. Having sent the last of her employees home ten minutes ago, Alexi now wandered alone around the room. It had long been her dream, but she hadn't realized how much pride she would feel when she finally had her own place. Ron had hired a decorator to help out with the design of the interior, and Alexi was pleased with the result. The dark woods and rich colors in the main room made the large space feel more intimate. In the back, a cluster of pool tables sat under stained-glass lamps, and four dart boards lined the walls.

Among the tastefully scattered sports memorabilia were several pieces from Alexi's own collection. A basketball signed by Magic Johnson that belonged to her father held a place of honor in a square case behind the bar. And because she knew he would have liked it, a display humidor with a mahogany finish and Spanish cedar trays held a selection of premium cigars. A familiar pang in her chest accompanied thoughts of her father, and as always, she wished he'd been around to see this place.

Alexi didn't need a shrink to tell her why creating the kind of upscale sports bar he would have frequented had still mattered to her a decade and a half after his death. Of course, she had spent so many years in between oblivious to just how many of her decisions had centered on her father's death.

Alexi glanced at a row of liquor bottles on a shelf behind the bar, and, though still present, the familiar urge to have a drink faded a bit every day. Whatever else had happened, she'd persevered, with some help from her friends, and now she had this place to show for it.

In the hazy light of early morning, a column of smoke wound above the city skyline. What less than an hour ago had been a thick, black plume had faded to a light gray. But Kate Chambers had been on enough fire scenes to imagine it as it had been. As she steered her Tahoe onto Fourth Avenue, her heartbeat accelerated at the cluster of fire apparatus parked in the street. The remembered rush of responding with lights and sirens to a scene sang through her blood. She parked next to the curb, and when she stepped out the familiar smell of smoke made heavy and humid by the water used to suppress the fire assailed her.

After grabbing a turnout coat, helmet, and flashlight from the truck she walked toward a group of firefighters clustered near one of the engines. The flames had nearly been extinguished, but a flurry of activity still surrounded the charred skeleton of the building that rose from the water-soaked debris. Unidentifiable men and women in turnout gear manned heavy lengths of hose around the perimeter of the building, and a couple of lines snaked inside the front door. Kate had listened to the radio on her way in and knew that a half hour earlier the district chief in charge had called for a defensive attack and all personnel had been withdrawn from the interior. Now that the fire had been knocked down, they were going back in to check for hot spots, areas still burning or smoldering.

The white shirt of the chief stood out among the smudged turnout coats. As Kate headed toward him, several firefighters stepped aside and she caught sight of her partner, Jason Hayworth, standing with him.

"Hey, Chambers." He glanced up from the notes he jotted in a spiral notebook. As she stopped beside him, she had to tilt her head back to meet his eyes. At five foot eleven, Kate was often as tall as most men, but Jason topped six feet by several inches. Add to that a broad chest, shaved head, thick black mustache, and deep voice, and he could be quite intimidating. Though Kate knew he was as gentle as a puppy, he'd told her that his imposing appearance often convinced witnesses to be straight with him. That was one tactic Kate wouldn't be able to employ. People tended to underestimate her because of her slim figure and blond hair.

"What have we got?" She slipped her flashlight under her arm and pulled out her own notebook.

"Looks like you drew a good first case. Sports bar. It went up quickly. I haven't been inside yet, but from what the chief is describing, I'd put money on an accelerant. The owners are on the way. We've got a witness over there." He gestured toward a woman talking to one of the firefighters. "You get her statement and I'll start talking to firefighters."

Kate nodded. In twelve years on an engine, she'd responded to countless scenes, but this was her first as an investigator. Jason had been with the fire marshal's office for eight years so she was glad he was there to guide her, especially if this one turned out to be arson.

As Kate approached, the witness looked at her nervously, wringing her hands and shifting her weight. Her hair was matted and pulled into a sloppy braid. Kate didn't even want to guess when the last time her layers of tattered clothing had been washed.

No doubt she was one of the group of homeless that lived under the nearby interstate overpass.

"Ma'am, can you tell me what you saw?" Kate clicked her pen.

"A black car." Her voice was rough and shaky.

"Could you tell what model?"

"I don't know nothing about cars. It was a black one's all I can say."

Kate nodded. That wasn't much help. "When did you see the car?"

"It drove off a few minutes before I smelled the smoke. Then I called 9-1-1 from that pay phone over there."

Kate glanced at the phone on the side of the vacant building across the street. It was covered in spray paint, and the metal shelf below the phone hung by one side as if someone had nearly succeeded in tearing it off. She was surprised the phone even worked.

"Which way did the car go?"

The woman pointed toward the interstate.

"And you didn't get a look at the driver?"

"I didn't know I needed to. It was gone by the time I realized there was a fire."

So not only was the black car not a good lead, it might not be one at all. Just because it was in the area a few minutes prior to the fire didn't mean the occupant was involved. Kate left the woman with her card and instructions to call if she remembered anything else. But she wouldn't wait for that call.

Minutes later, as she relayed the witness's statement to Jason, Kate was surprised to see a black Cadillac park behind her Tahoe. The driver's door opened and an African American woman stepped out. Her tan overcoat hung open to reveal baggy jeans and a wrinkled T-shirt. Her hair was extremely short, merely an ebony cap that enhanced her angular features. She looked at the remains of the building, then away quickly. Her eyes darted among the people moving about the scene until they locked on

Kate's, and Kate felt the connection like a hand reaching into her chest. As the woman drew near, she continued to hold Kate's gaze, worry evident in her dark brown eyes.

"What happened?" she demanded. Her brows drew together, marring otherwise smooth skin.

"There was a fire." Jason stated the obvious. "Are you the owner?"

"One of them. Alexi Clark," she answered, without taking her eyes from Kate's face. "My business partner is on his way. Do you know what caused the fire?"

"Not yet, Ms. Clark. Maybe you can help us with that. Is that your car?" He pointed at the Cadillac.

"Of course it's my car."

"Did anyone borrow it earlier?"

"No." She glanced between Kate and Jason. "What's going on?"

"Alexi! Alexi, what happened?" a man shouted as he rushed toward them.

"That's my partner, Ron Volk."

"You finish up here," Jason said to Kate as he moved to intercept the approaching man.

Kate nodded, knowing he would want to question Mr. Volk and Ms. Clark separately.

"It's all gone," Alexi said quietly as Jason walked away.

Her eyes filled with tears as she stared at what was left of her business. Kate had recognized the stark sense of loss on the faces of property owners before, but something about seeing it on Alexi's strong features made Kate think she should look away, as if she was invading Alexi's privacy. Kate's chest ached and she finally did angle herself toward the scene, needing to escape the heartbreak emanating from Alexi.

"By the time the firefighters arrived they weren't able to save your bar—"

"In Left Field."

"What?"

"That's what it's called. In Left Field."

"Okay. Do you have any idea how the fire may have started?"

"No." Alexi whispered so softly Kate barely heard her.

Kate lifted her hand then jerked it back, realizing she'd been about to touch Alexi's shoulder. She pulled her pen from her shirt pocket in an effort to cover the motion.

Those dark eyes met Kate's again, determination shining through her pain. "Can I go inside?"

"No. We can't let you in until we've completed our investigation."

"What's your name?" Alexi snapped.

"Kate Chambers. I'm an investigator with the fire department."

"Well, Ms. Chambers, that's my whole life in there. I just want to see if there's anything left." When tears spilled over high cheekbones, she swiped at them angrily and turned her head away as if she didn't want Kate to see them.

"I understand. But we can't risk any potential evidence being disturbed." Kate shifted uncomfortably. More accustomed to working with the crews packing up gear around them, she still hadn't adjusted to her new role. But she was positive that no one was allowed inside until they finished documenting the scene.

Alexi jerked her head back to meet Kate's eyes. "You think this was arson?"

"It looks that way. Where were you this morning?"

"At home in bed."

"Alone?"

"What business is that of yours?" Alexi's tone was defensive, but Kate would make no apologies for doing her job.

"Is there anyone who can verify your whereabouts?"

"No."

"What time did you get home?"

"I closed last night. So, I guess I was probably home by three thirty."

"You don't know?"

"Three thirty or quarter till four."

"What about Mr. Volk, when was the last time you saw him?" Jason and Ron stood near Kate's Tahoe. Ron pushed up his glasses and glanced at Alexi as he spoke. Alexi looked up, and though Kate's attention never left Alexi, she could tell by the stiffening of Alexi's posture that their gaze met. Kate searched Alexi's face for some hint of communication between the two of them, but none was evident.

"I sent him home around midnight."

"He didn't close up with you."

"No." Alexi still watched Ron and Jason. "Business was slow, so I told him to go."

"Are the two of you usually so involved in the day-to-day operations?"

When Alexi turned back to Kate, her expression was immediately wary. "It's not uncommon. Usually there's a lot of administrative stuff that gets our attention first. But we were short-handed last night, so we both pitched in."

"We need a list of your employees. And I'd like to know which ones worked last night, or were supposed to and didn't show."

"I can give you names, but Ron should have a complete personnel roster, with addresses and phone numbers. I imagine you'll want that as well."

"Please. If you could, note which employees have keys to the building. Do you have an alarm system?"

"Yes."

"Was it armed?"

Alexi nodded.

Kate made a note to check with the monitoring company. "Is there anyone who might have a grudge against you or Mr. Volk?"

Alexi stared at the investigator, hearing her words but struggling to absorb their meaning. It hadn't occurred to Alexi that the fire was anything more than an accident. She'd imagined the worst when she'd been summoned downtown only hours after closing the bar. But still she'd been unprepared for the horror of seeing her livelihood reduced to ash.

"Ma'am."

It took Alexi a moment to realize that Kate Chambers was talking to her. Alexi shook her head, forcing herself to pay attention to what Kate had asked. Was there really a chance the fire was set intentionally? Electrical problems, maybe. But arson? What was it Chambers had asked her? Did anyone have a grudge against Alexi or Ron?

"No." Alexi shook her head. "I don't know anyone who would do this." She met Chambers's gaze once again, struggling to focus on something besides the surreal events moving around her. Her stomach clenched painfully. Shock and adrenaline were the only things that kept her from dropping to her knees and vomiting.

The investigator was tall, matching Alexi's nearly six-foot frame. Eye to eye, Alexi could see that Chambers's irises were the clearest green she'd ever seen, bringing to mind the waters of Florida's Emerald Coast. Pale blond hair was drawn back tightly from her face and into a bun at the base of her neck, and her equally light brows were shaped into delicate arcs. Aside from the uniform, she didn't look like a firefighter. With a classic, runway-worthy bone structure, she was an attractive package, but Alexi's interest lasted only as long as it took her to figure out she was on this woman's list of suspects.

"Listen, it'll probably be a few hours before we can let you inside, maybe you should—"

"I'm not going anywhere until I've had a chance to examine my bar." Alexi was surprised to see understanding seep into Chambers's expression.

"There's a coffee shop across the street. You might be more comfortable waiting there."

Alexi folded her arms across her chest. "I'll wait right here."

"Suit yourself."

CHAPTER TWO

"What do you think?" Kate asked as she joined Jason next to their Tahoes. Twenty feet away, Ron Volk bent his head to speak quietly to Alexi Clark.

"His wife is his alibi, but I haven't ruled him out yet." He opened the back hatch of the vehicle, then reached inside and pulled out several empty paint-can-shaped containers used to store evidence.

"Ms. Clark doesn't have an alibi. At home in bed alone."

"I need to get statements from the guys on Truck 3. Would you start photographing the exterior?" The truck crew had been responsible for ventilation, and they needed to account for any windows they had broken. Then Kate and Jason could try to determine which, if any, the suspect had smashed and which the fire had damaged.

"Got it." Kate grabbed a canvas bag from her SUV and slung it over her shoulder. She reached back in for a square, hard-shelled case.

"After we get the scene documented, we'll head back to the office and start looking into their personal information."

From the bag hanging near her hip, Kate pulled a Nikon D300, one of a dozen cameras purchased by the department when they made the switch to digital. She affixed the flash and took a couple of shots of the front of the business. As she rounded the northeast corner, the building blocked the light from the streetlamp. Kate turned on her flashlight as she searched the shadows close to the building and picked her way carefully over sodden ground pockmarked with footprints from the heavy boots of dozens of firefighters. Any evidence of a fleeing suspect most likely had been eradicated this close to the building.

She photographed shards of glass outside one of the windows and a segment of the brick wall that had collapsed at the back of the structure. After pulling on latex gloves, she collected the glass for analysis. None of the exterior window frames showed signs of forced entry. She circled the building, documenting the area from all angles to aid them in diagramming the scene later.

As she reached the front once more, Jason walked toward her. Behind him, crews continued to pack up equipment and roll hose. A ladder truck eased carefully away from the curb and around the other apparatus. Kate automatically checked the company numbers on the side of the vehicles, looking for her old crew.

Jason pulled out a small flashlight. “Let’s go inside.”

The bar’s brick façade still stood, like the false front of a Hollywood film set, making unfulfilled promises about what they might find inside. They stepped carefully over the threshold and began to pick their way through debris. Sections of the roof had collapsed and burned, and firefighters had ripped down others searching for pockets of smoldering embers. Larger structure fires often resulted in engines being called back out hours later for a rekindle when one of these hidden hot spots ignited again.

As they entered, they followed the north wall toward the back of the bar, documenting anything notable, either on paper or photographically. They began their search in a spiral pattern that would end in the center of the room.

Kate paused near the same window where she’d collected the glass fragments earlier. Squatting down, she focused the camera and took several shots of a pile of soggy gypsum board.

“What have you got?” Jason asked.

Kate carefully lifted away a triangle of sheetrock to reveal a fist-sized chunk of concrete.

"Looks like a piece of a curb or sidewalk."

Kate nodded.

Jason glanced at the broken window then back at the floor. "What's missing?"

Kate could tell from his tone that he already knew and was testing her. "Well, it *looks* like the concrete chunk was thrown through the window. Forced entry." She paused and watched his expression change to one of disappointment. "*But*, there's no glass on the floor. If the window was broken from the outside, the glass would be in here, not on the ground outside, which is where I found it. So, this was planted here and the window was broken from inside."

"Right. Collect the concrete."

They continued to circle the room, working toward the remains of the bar stretching along the back. Jason pointed out burn patterns on the walls, and Kate photographed everything he showed her. They wouldn't need all of the shots for evidence in the case, but Kate wanted to study them later. She was training herself to see and interpret the patterns on her own.

They found the most damage in the back third of the building, indicating the fire started there. The bar was destroyed, consumed almost beyond recognition by the flames. Broken and distorted glass covered the counter behind it, and Kate could imagine the rows of liquor bottles that once stood there.

Jason knelt in front of the bar. "Look at this."

Kate joined him. The hardwood floor was heavily blackened, but an asymmetrical area in the middle was slightly lighter than that around it. "Could be a liquid accelerant."

Jason nodded. "Maybe. But responders reported a flashover shortly after they arrived on scene so we can't assume it's accelerant pooling. We'll take a sample." The extreme heat generated when all the combustible material in the room had ignited could cause uneven burn patterns as well.

Jason pulled a hammer and chisel from his kit while Kate snapped a few pictures of the charred shape. Kate set down her camera and opened one of the paint cans.

"When you pull a sample, you need to make sure you go deep enough to get below the char line," Jason explained while he pried up a sample of the floor. "Since there was a witness who can give us an approximate time the fire started, I don't think we'll need to measure the depth. But it's better to have it and not need it."

Kate remembered from her classroom lectures that most materials burned at predictable rates and measuring the char depth could help an investigator approximate the time of ignition. The cross-section Jason placed in the can included the hardwood plank and several inches of subfloor.

They continued their search, ending in the center section where firefighters had piled many of the burned-up tables and chairs.

"I never gave much thought to evidence while I was in here throwing furniture around," Kate mused while they carefully lifted away each piece.

"I never did either. Most don't. It really takes seeing the incident from another perspective to realize how important it is to be careful."

"There's a balance, isn't there? During suppression, our priority is finding the fire. But you guys need to keep as much evidence undisturbed as possible."

"It's not 'you guys' anymore. You're one of us now."

Whether she liked it or not.

"I'm just saying, she's hot, but not Halle Berry hot," Jason said over his shoulder as he walked into the old brick building that used to house fire headquarters. When the other administrative offices had been moved into a new building, the arson division had been left behind. The eight investigators shared one large office, each with a battered metal desk. A conference room adjoined the space and held several tables where investigators sorted evidence before they sent it off for lab analysis.

"Well, who is? Aren't you married, anyway?"

"Married. Not dead."

Kate didn't quite agree with Jason's assessment of Alexi Clark. She wasn't soft enough to pull off feminine, and she'd triggered more than a gentle ping on Kate's gaydar. But she did have a trim, athletic body and full mouth that had pouted slightly then tightened when she tried not to cry as she stared at the remains of her bar. Kate caught herself before she could think too long about whether those lips would feel as soft as they looked. Regardless, Kate would choose Alexi Clark over Halle Berry any day.

"Anyway, she's a suspect, so how hot she is or isn't doesn't matter." Although Jason probably didn't realize it, the reminder was for herself as much as for him. As far as she knew, he assumed she was straight. She didn't usually talk about her sex life with her crewmates. She figured some of them drew their own conclusions, but she didn't substantiate them. And, she reluctantly admitted, there hadn't been much to talk about lately anyway. Her last serious relationship had been over a year ago, and since then she hadn't had the energy for dating.

The office was uncharacteristically empty. Kate had heard another call go out for two of the other investigators while she and Jason were finishing up at In Left Field. And Branagh and Walsh had been in and out of the office while working a massive warehouse fire from two days ago.

Jason set a box containing their evidence on his desk, and Kate placed hers next to it.

"You're right. But I'm a guy, Kate, and that means whether it matters or not, how hot she is still registers in my brain." He dropped into his chair. "Damn, I feel like I need a shower."

"You do." Soot and dust streaked his white shirt, and a

smudge slashed across his forehead where he'd obviously swiped at sweat.

"Let's go get cleaned up and then we'll get to work on these reports."

They had spent the morning thoroughly documenting the scene before returning to the office. Now they had several hours of paperwork ahead of them sifting through evidence and beginning to pull together background information on the owners and employees of the bar. They would be much more comfortable if they freshened up.

"Pizza for lunch?" Jason asked as together they headed for the sleeping quarters at the end of the hallway. It was little more than a storage room with several cots and a row of lockers jammed into it.

"We had pizza Monday. You know I don't like to eat the same thing twice in one week."

"That rule of yours is crazy."

Kate grinned at Jason, knowing he would defer to her on this. "It's a rule nonetheless. Chinese?"

"All right. But I get the extra egg roll." Jason took a clean uniform and a toiletry bag from his locker.

"Deal." Kate draped her own clothes over her arm. "I'll meet you up front in fifteen," she said as she pushed through the door to the women's restroom.

Once inside, she stepped into the dressing area of one of the shower stalls and quickly stripped off her uniform. She'd always been the type to linger in a hot shower, then take her time dressing and putting on makeup. She was the last one ready to go anywhere, and her friends joked about how long it took. But out of necessity, after only a week in the academy she'd pared her preparation time down. She still made sure not a strand of her blond hair was out of place and her face was properly made up, but she'd learned to do so more efficiently. Her obvious vanity coupled with her thin build sometimes made her a target for her fellow trainees' ribbing. Even the instructors didn't seem to take her seriously as a firefighting candidate, so she'd worked even harder to prove that she wanted the job.

Twelve minutes later, with three to spare, Kate looked at her reflection in the mirror as she smoothed a hand over a tight French braid. She refused to compromise attention to detail for time constraints. She grabbed her purse and headed back to the outer room to stow her gear in her locker.

When she returned to her desk, Jason was already seated with the phone wedged between his ear and shoulder.

"Kung Pao chicken and…" He gave her a questioning look.

"Beef and broccoli."

"Beef and broccoli. Egg rolls and extra duck sauce, please."

Kate sat at her desk and turned on the monitor for her desktop. She removed the memory card from her camera and pushed it in the dedicated slot on the computer. Then she copied the photos from the scene into a new folder, identified by the case number, and backed them up on an external hard drive. As she browsed the pictures she selected several to print.

When the shot she'd taken of Alexi's Cadillac flashed on the screen, Kate paused to study it. The car matched the description of the vehicle seen fleeing the scene. And, Kate told herself, that was her only reason for snapping the photo. At the time, she'd barely noticed the figure leaning against the front near the tire. Alexi had waited there, arms and ankles crossed, while Kate and Jason finished examining the scene. While Kate had been concentrating on her work, she had been able to ignore Alexi's presence, but now as she mentally reviewed their conversation, she could pinpoint the moment Alexi realized she could be a suspect.

The surge of defensiveness in Alexi's demeanor had disappointed Kate. She immediately shook away that thought. Even if they ruled Alexi out as a suspect, she was still part of a case, and that meant Kate's interest should only be professional. It shouldn't matter that seeing Alexi's wounded eyes well up as she stared at the bar had nearly inspired Kate to touch her—to offer comfort.

Chapter Three

Alexi shoved open the door of her apartment and shrugged out of her coat in the foyer. Eager to cleanse herself of the smell of stale smoke that clung to her, she headed straight for the bathroom. She and Ron had waited impatiently for several hours until they had been cleared to go inside the bar. When he attempted to convince her to go home and come back later, she refused. She was not about to leave until those investigators finished searching her property and she could see the damage for herself. She wasn't sure which tortured her more, the waiting or actually going inside and facing the destruction.

After she showered and dressed in clean cargo pants and a rust-colored T-shirt, Alexi wandered into the living room. Her calico, Jack, wound between her legs and she bent to scratch his head.

"Hey, there, did you miss me?" Jack allowed the attention for only a minute, then tossed his head as if throwing off her caress and walked away. He settled on the window seat across the room, his attention on something on the other side of the glass. "Apparently not."

Alexi was convinced Jack merely tolerated her, and to be fair she wasn't exactly a cat person either. One of her waitresses had found him, dirty and emaciated, by the dumpster behind the bar one night, and somehow Alexi had been guilted into taking him home. Since then they'd co-existed in her loft with Jack mostly ignoring her unless she had an open can of cat food in her hand.

For nearly a decade, Alexi had rented one-bedroom apartments in order to save as much of her salary as she could for the bar. Frugality had become such a habit that even when she could afford it, signing the more expensive lease on this converted loft over a law firm had made her nervous. Downtown real estate was pricey, so she had sacrificed space to find a place she could afford that was only a few blocks from the bar. What it lacked in square footage, it made up in character. Cherry hardwood floors and matching molding added richness, and sizeable windows along the south wall kept the room from becoming too dark. Overlooking Commerce Street, she had a nice view of the Ryman Auditorium.

But today, as Alexi crossed the room, she was too distracted to appreciate that view. The buildings on Broadway made it impossible for her to see her bar only a few blocks south. *Or what's left of my bar.* This morning, she had driven there in a panic that turned to blinding pain when she turned the corner and first glimpsed the building. As she'd stepped from the car, her world tilted in the eerie red flashing lights of the countless fire trucks. She'd cast about for an anchor and found it momentarily when her gaze locked on Kate Chambers. It wasn't until they spoke and Kate made her not-so-veiled accusations that the inexplicable connection splintered and Alexi was left alone amid her nightmare once again.

She strode away from the window, angry at the reminder of forces she couldn't control. She couldn't sit here alone, brooding. Eager to escape, she grabbed her jacket and keys and took the back stairs to the parking lot below. The Cadillac sat just outside the door in one of two reserved spots assigned to Alexi. The remainder of the spaces belonged to the law firm, and downtown parking was at such a premium that the partners diligently policed the lot.

Once inside the car, Alexi steered into the grid of one-way streets that made up the heart of the city. Alexi had grown up in a suburb of Nashville and could negotiate the confusing maze with ease. She remembered as a child coming into the city with her parents to see a show at TPAC. She always felt special seated between them with a box of popcorn in her lap and would easily get lost in the moment when the lights dimmed and the first strains of music swelled. Sometimes she wished it was still that easy to escape from real life, even if just for a couple of hours.

After her parents' divorce, her mother dragged her in to see the ballet, and her father won her over with season tickets to Vanderbilt basketball. Their lives became a competition for Alexi's affection, and her father always came out on top. Alexi was never interested in the girlie things her mother suggested. She was much happier on the weekends when she could go to the ball game or a car show with her father.

But, as confusing as this tug-of-war was at times, she couldn't blame her problems on her parents' split. She'd had a typical upbringing for her generation; most of her peers were also children of divorce. She'd been an athlete and a *B* student, and had partied with her friends to escape her not-so-cool parents. During her senior year in high school she confessed to a crush on her best friend and discovered that her feelings were reciprocated. Thus began her first and longest relationship with a woman.

Her partying had escalated as she entered college. When she was drinking, Alexi was able to let loose and be what she considered a more fun version of herself. Though Alexi's social habits sometimes put a strain on her relationship with her girlfriend, she was always able to apologize and gain forgiveness for whatever offense she committed.

But after college, Alexi had a life-changing experience that she didn't come out on the positive side of. Her father passed away and she entered the darkest period of her life, the shadows of which still clung to her insides.

❖

"I've been waiting for you," Danielle, Ron's wife and Alexi's best friend, said as she swung open the front door of their condo.

"How did you know I would come here?"

"When you're upset you brood for a while and then you need to talk." Danielle wrapped an arm around Alexi's waist and guided her inside. "Come in, I'm making tea."

"I don't know what I'd do without you," Alexi muttered.

"You never need to find out."

Alexi allowed Danielle to lead her into the kitchen and settled on a stool at the island as Danielle pulled a tin of peppermint herbal tea and two mugs from the cabinet.

"Are you okay, honey?" The concern in Danielle's voice had Alexi tearing up.

They'd been through some tough times, and Danielle had always been there even when Alexi didn't deserve it. She'd thought she was going to lose her once and still wondered if she could ever make amends for the times she'd abused their friendship. She would shut Danielle out one day, then call her in a depressed stupor the next. Danielle always showed up to clean Alexi up and get her through another day. The one exception had been immediately following her father's death. After the funeral, she got in her car and drove until she couldn't see through her tears, then checked into a motel off the interstate. She holed up in a room there and didn't answer her cell phone for a week. When she finally returned home, Danielle wouldn't speak to her. It had taken a lot of groveling and a promise that she would never scare her like that again before Danielle finally forgave her.

And now, as the pressure of this day closed in on Alexi, she hoped her friend's presence could steady her again. She'd come here because she knew Danielle would take care of her.

"I'm not okay," Alexi answered. She was uncomfortable

letting her emotions flow this close to the surface, but her usual means of anesthetizing them was no longer an option. "What are we going to do?" Alexi rubbed a trembling hand across her forehead. When she thought about how hard they would have to work to rebuild their business, her head ached and her stomach felt queasy.

Danielle reached across the counter and covered Alexi's hand. "We'll get through this."

Alexi tried to smile. It was no wonder the three of them made such a good business team. Alexi had the operations knowledge and Ron the business mind, but they both relied on Danielle's nurturing optimism. The strength of their bonds to Danielle held their partnership together even when they disagreed.

"The fire department is saying it was arson. And that investigator seemed to think I had something to do with it."

Danielle waved a hand dismissively. "They have to look at you guys first. As soon as they figure out both of you are innocent, they'll move on." She set a mug in front of Alexi, then circled the bar to sit beside her.

"I'm losing my mind here, Danielle. I can't forget that smell, when I first stepped out of the car." Just talking about the moment brought it rushing back with vivid clarity. The acrid smell had assaulted her. Not the pleasant smoky scent of a campfire, but a sharp odor that burned the back of her throat and made her eyes water.

"I know, sweetie." Danielle wrapped an arm around Alexi's shoulder. "Uh, have you been to a meeting lately?"

"Subtle."

"What, I can't worry about you? This is a stressful time and—"

"And I'm handling it."

"Okay, okay." Danielle eased her arm away and folded her manicured hands together in front of her. Even when obviously worried about Ron and Alexi, Danielle was perfectly primped.

Flawless makeup covered the tiny lines the years had left in her caramel complexion, and every strand of ebony hair remained in place.

"How's Ron doing?"

"He came home long enough to make a few phone calls, then went back out. You know how he is. He doesn't talk to me when he's upset about something."

Ron's inability to open up emotionally had been the major source of conflict in their marriage, and had gotten worse in recent months. Danielle had confided in Alexi that he'd agreed to counseling only after she threatened to leave him, but he was showing no sign of letting her in, and Danielle often complained that she ended up at the counseling sessions by herself.

Alexi covered Danielle's hand. "I wish there was something I could do."

"He's so distant. You would think I would know how to handle that type of behavior in my life by now."

"He just needs time." The reference to her own inability to let anyone close hit home, and Alexi found herself defending Ron. Their shared tendency to shut down emotionally was the one area where Alexi was more like Ron than Danielle.

"The funny thing is, he thinks he's hiding it from me. I know something's going on, but he won't talk to me about it."

Alexi hesitated. She had some concerns about Ron's activities of late, but was unsure how much Danielle knew about his dealings. She didn't want to broach a subject that would exacerbate their already unsteady relationship until she had more concrete questions. She needed more time before she could begin to think clearly. Instead she simply said, "I need to figure out what happened at the bar last night."

"Didn't you say there was an investigator doing that? Ron said the insurance company has to wait for their report before they can cut a check."

Alexi pushed away her untouched tea and sighed in

frustration. “Well, in the meantime, I can’t sit around and do nothing. I’ll go insane.”

“What choice do you have?”

“I’ll do some investigating of my own.”

“That’s not a good idea.” Shaking her head, Danielle stood and put their mugs in the sink.

“Relax, Danielle. I’m not planning to do anything crazy, maybe just ask a few questions. I need to feel like I’m doing something. Besides, the sooner this is settled the better. Preferably before our employees find jobs they like better. We’re already going to lose some time rebuilding. I don’t want to have to train an all-new staff as well.”

“You should leave the investigating to the professionals. There are other things you could do to fill your time. Why don’t you see if you can pick up a few shifts at the Blue Line?”

“I’ll think about it.” The Blue Line, a popular cop bar, was owned by an old friend of Alexi’s father, and if she asked he would let her tend bar there a few nights a week. The activity would help take her mind off things. Past experience had shown that she got into trouble when she stayed idle.

❖

“So suddenly my three-year-old began speaking fluent Russian.”

“Uh-huh.”

“Kate.”

“What?” She looked up from the computer screen she’d just read for the third time.

“You haven’t heard a word I’ve said.” Irritation colored Jason’s voice.

“Yes, I have. Your three-year-old speaks Russian.” Kate paused as the words she’d absently repeated registered. “Really?”

"Yes. He's a prodigy," Jason deadpanned. "Did you catch anything before that?"

Kate shook her head guiltily.

"You're a million miles away. Something wrong?"

"No. I'm just a little distracted."

"You just got your first case yesterday, and your next won't be far behind. You can't afford distraction." Jason smiled despite his critical words.

"Sorry." He was right. She'd been warned she would carry several cases simultaneously. Some, of course, would be simple minor property damage, easily resolved, and others would be more complicated. But cases were assigned on a rotating basis, and since no one could predict when the next fire would be, their workload would fluctuate.

She rubbed a hand against her jaw and pulled a legal pad closer. She'd been running on the adrenaline of her first case as an investigator since the previous morning when she first arrived on scene. Sleep had come slowly last night, and the alarm had sounded way too early this morning. She would crash eventually, but she needed to get several more hours of work in first.

Intent on salvaging as much concentration as she could, she grabbed her mouse and clicked through several screens. She'd been reading old newspaper articles, beginning with those that chronicled the opening of a new sports bar, In Left Field, and ending with a story about yesterday's fire. The first story told of a new partnership—Alexi Clark and investor Ron Volk had purchased a building in dubious condition on what could be a prime location. The reporter had interviewed other downtown business owners who were mostly of the opinion that the area couldn't support another sports bar. But, the article went on to say, Ms. Clark was unconcerned, stating emphatically that her bar would set itself apart as a classy yet comfortable place to gather and watch the big games. Kate had never been there, but some of her peers had described it as just that.

As Kate progressed through the years, she could almost

see Alexi's bar ingratiate itself into the community. There were photos of the grand opening, a smiling Alexi cutting a ribbon and drawing the first draft from the tap behind the bar. The next year, In Left Field sponsored a co-ed softball team, and though they lost the championship game, they didn't seem to mind as they toasted the camera with foam-capped mugs. She skimmed articles about charity fundraisers and game-night specials. With each one, Alexi proved her skeptics wrong as her sports bar carved out a niche.

"Our bar owners were in financial trouble."

"What?" Kate jerked her head up.

Jason leaned closer to his monitor and squinted slightly. Money was one of the top motives for arson. Jason had been in contact with the district attorney's office that morning and had secured a warrant for the bar's financial records. "Yeah, from the looks of this report, if things didn't change, by the end of the year they needed to seriously think about getting out."

"That doesn't make any sense. Everything I've found indicates it was a popular place." Somehow "financially irresponsible" didn't fit Kate's impression of Alexi, which was silly considering she didn't know the woman well enough to gauge accurately. But the profile of Alexi she'd been building since the moment they'd met told her that In Left Field meant far too much for Alexi to endanger its future.

"Oh, they were making money. But what I can't figure out is, once a week for the past three months there's a large withdrawal from their business account. It doesn't match up with any of their operating expenses."

"How large?" Jason turned his computer screen toward her and Kate scanned the numbers.

"Are both their names on the account?" Kate tried to rationalize the kernel of hope that Alexi was not involved in whatever trouble her bar was in. She was simply trying to be as thorough in their investigation as possible.

For several long moments the only sound in the room was

the click of Jason's mouse. Finally, he answered, "Yes. And Ron's wife as well."

"Can we find out which one of them is taking it out?"

"I'll look into it." Jason's attention continued to swing between the computer screen in front of him and the notebook to the right of his keyboard. "But these aren't small numbers, Kate. I don't see how either of them could be in the dark about the shortages."

"Maybe they were all in on it."

"If his wife was involved, Mr. Volk's alibi is suddenly a bit shaky. Why don't you take a pass at the wife?"

"I'll call her today."

Kate continued to wade through newspaper articles until the words started to blur. She shoved her chair back and spun around to face Jason. "Do you mind if I take a break?"

He waved a hand toward the door without looking up. "Bring back lunch. Sandwiches."

"I know just the place." Kate couldn't get out of the room fast enough. They'd been searching paperwork all morning, and she wasn't yet accustomed to spending this much time behind a desk. She needed some air and her restless muscles needed to move.

Kate pulled her Tahoe into the parking lot of Station 18, one of forty located throughout the county. She turned off the ignition, but instead of getting out, she sat and stared at the station where she'd spent every third day for most of her tenure with the department. The exterior was unremarkable, red brick with two large truck bays and sparse landscaping. A basketball goal had been erected at one end of the parking lot, and Kate had won more games of Horse than she'd lost under that hoop. Inside Kate knew the layout well: the living quarters and kitchen spanned the front, the sleeping area and offices were tucked in the back.

As a firefighter assigned to Engine 18 she'd worked twenty-four-hour shifts with forty-eight hours off in between. But ten weeks ago, the course of her career had changed. While at a house fire, she and two of her crewmates were running hose around the side of the building when an exterior wall collapsed. Kate had been pulled from the rubble unconscious and remained so for almost thirty-six hours.

When doctors said her back injury would likely end her career as a firefighter, Kate refused to believe them. She barely took a moment for self-pity before she immersed herself in physical therapy, with no luck. She'd regained her mobility and most of her strength, but couldn't get clearance to go back to full duty. If it hadn't been for her chief's endorsement to the fire marshal's office, she might have ended up a glorified secretary in an administrative office. She spent a week wallowing and threatening to leave the department altogether before she finally put away the ice-cream carton and turned off the Lifetime movies. When she was able to think clearly again, she accepted the position as an investigator.

"Do you intend to sit out here all day?"

Kate smiled even before she turned to look at the woman standing outside her passenger window. "I was thinking about it. You didn't know you had a stalker, did you?"

"Baby, I wish I had a stalker." Paula Stocks, Kate's closest friend in the department, made up one half of the best paramedic crew in the city. She pulled open Kate's door. "Get out."

When Kate obeyed, Paula swept her into a tight hug, then released her almost as quickly. Side by side they walked toward the building, and as they rounded the corner a hulking man stood up from the park bench situated under the shade of a large elm.

"Hey, kid. How are you?" He was affectionately referred to as Bear, and lived up to that name in both height and breadth.

Kate grinned as he slapped her roughly on the shoulder. "I'm good, man. I figured you'd be missing me by now."

"Yeah, we thought you were too good for us now. Whatcha been up to?"

"Four weeks of rehab for the back. Then training for this investigator gig. I kept meaning to visit, but you know how that goes."

"Sure thing. It's great to see you now though."

Paula touched Kate's arm. "Come on inside. We've got some catching up to do."

"Don't be a stranger, kid."

Kate shook Bear's hand, then followed Paula. She waited until they were well inside before she said, "That guy couldn't stand me when I first got here, and now he misses me like crazy?"

"You know what they say about absence."

"Paula, he constantly acted like I was some weak girl who had no business doing this job."

They entered the otherwise empty living room and Paula dropped down on the sofa. Kate perched on the arm of a nearby chair.

"But you proved yourself."

"I shouldn't have had to. You didn't."

"Well, look at me, Kate." Paula swept a hand over her reclined body. Her broad shoulders, muscular thighs, and thick waist left little doubt as to her strength. "I'm built like a frigging trucker."

Kate always hated to hear her friend put herself down this way. But she'd accepted that Paula didn't consider her strong, pure heart a fair trade-off for a lack of classic beauty a long time ago. "Paula—"

"I mean, shit, you look like a model. Besides, I'm a paramedic. Guys like Bear think the only place a woman belongs is in the medical service."

"I can't believe you're condoning this double standard." Even now, ten years after Kate's days as a rookie, women in the fire service had to work harder to earn the respect of their peers than their EMS counterparts. Since some recent promotions had moved a woman into the upper echelon of leadership, Kate was hopeful that things would change someday.

Paula leaned forward and steel gray eyes met Kate's. "I'm not condoning anything. But this isn't about equality in the workplace. We don't have an office job. These guys have to know they can put their lives in your hands."

"Well, there's no need to worry about that anymore." Kate couldn't keep the bitterness out of her voice. She might complain about the disparity to Paula, but she never used it as excuse not to do her job. She simply proved to the men that she could work as hard and as long as they could. Now she would be using a whole new skill set, one that had nothing to do with brawn. And though maybe she should have felt some relief at that change, she didn't.

"So that's what this visit is about, you're feeling sorry for yourself."

"Wouldn't you? I've got a couple decades of basically sitting behind a desk to look forward to until I can retire." Hopelessness settled in her stomach. She'd been playing the same scenario in her head for weeks and simply couldn't visualize her new career path.

"I thought you were past the pity parties."

Paula had been there for Kate after her injury. She'd sat at Kate's bedside when she awakened and, later, had driven her to physical therapy when Kate couldn't stand her mother's hovering any longer. After her injury, Kate's mother hadn't missed an opportunity to remind Kate that she'd predicted precisely such an incident when Kate insisted on going into the academy. She worried enough about her husband and son, but a woman had no business being a firefighter.

Paula had been Kate's only contact with the outside world and the reason Kate was able to hold onto her sanity. She had even patiently endured Kate's agony over her future. Whenever Kate had a bad day and questioned why she was working so hard just to get behind a desk, Paula had reminded her that a lot of people had a much tougher life than she did.

"I thought I was past those pitiful parties too. But what you're doing—it has purpose. You're saving lives. What am I doing? Helping settle insurance claims?"

"Sweetie, is there any chance you'll get back on an engine someday?" Paula touched Kate's arm as if to take the sting out of the question only she could get away with asking—the question to which she already knew the answer.

But for Kate no amount of comfort could soothe the barb of knowing that her life would never be what she wanted it to be again. Kate didn't normally succumb to such flashes of drama, but recently she hadn't been able to reconcile herself to her fate. "That's the kicker. As long as I don't do any heavy lifting I feel great. But the doc says if I go back out, it's only a matter of time before I reinjure myself, maybe even worse."

"And you've finally decided to listen to the doctor's advice."

"I don't want to. But let's say I somehow get back on an engine. What if I'm carrying someone out, a citizen or someone in my own crew, and I get hurt again. If I'm not able to save someone—I'm not sure I could live with that kind of guilt. Like you said, those guys put their lives in our hands, and being on an engine when I can't even trust myself wouldn't be right."

"Then you really have two choices. Figure out how to find meaning in what you're doing now or do something else."

"Just go do something else? It's not that easy."

"Sure it is. People change careers all the time."

"Because they want to, not because they have to." With a sigh of frustration, she slid off the arm and into the chair. "I'd feel differently if this had been my choice."

"Come on, Kate, you're not the first person to get a raw deal. We all play the hand we're dealt. You're being a bit of a whiner."

Kate stared at her. She could always count on Paula for unapologetic honesty.

A sweep of ebony hair fell across Paula's face and she shoved it back, but Kate wasn't sure if the impatient gesture was meant for the lock of hair or for Kate. "It sounds like you need a night out to take your mind off things. What are you doing tonight? How long has it been since we hung out and had a few drinks?"

"Too long." Kate glanced at her watch. She'd been gone from the office for thirty minutes. "I have to get back soon."

"Are we on for tonight, then?"

"Sure, why not."

"The Blue Line at nine?"

"See you then. And thanks."

Kate strode through the fire station, then the truck bay, letting her fingers graze the side of the engine as she passed. Paula was right. Dwelling on what she couldn't have any longer wouldn't do any good. She only hoped she stopped feeling that pang of loss and envy someday.

CHAPTER FOUR

Alexi swiped a towel over the bar, mopping up water rings from the scarred wooden surface.

"Can I have another beer, sweetheart."

Despite this being Alexi's first shift at the Blue Line, she'd already identified the gravel-voiced man perched at the corner of the bar as a regular. A cop, probably retired, he had the weary eyes of a career patrol officer. She ignored the endearment and pulled another draft.

"You new here?" He slurred his words as she placed the mug in front of him.

"Yes."

"Good. We need some young blood around this dive."

"Sorry, buddy. I'm just temporary." Alexi turned away without waiting for a response.

It hadn't taken long for her to determine that two types of officers frequented the bar—the retirees who showed up in early afternoon and those still on the job who came in after their shifts to drink away the fumes that the worst of humanity left on them every day. The remainder of the clientele consisted of firefighters, paramedics, and a few stray civilians.

Alexi appreciated the distraction of being behind the bar again, but she missed the familiar surroundings of her own place. She even missed her most demanding regulars. Crazy as it seemed, she actually wondered what bartender was now serving dry martinis to Trish Langley and whether she sent as many back as she had to Alexi.

The stools opposite her had been filling up rapidly over the past several hours, but the sedate older men perched there couldn't compete with the group of young men and women who occupied five of the tables in the back of the room. They had come in about an hour ago and were rapidly consuming tequila shots. The volume of their laughter escalated in direct proportion to the number of drinks Alexi sent over.

The waitress responsible for the raucous crowd rounded the bar. She slid an empty tray onto the surface and sighed. "I need another round of shooters." A roar rose up from across the room as if to punctuate the request.

"What the hell is going on over there?" Alexi filled the tray with shot glasses.

"Fire-academy graduation."

"Quite the celebration," Alexi mused as the waitress carefully balanced the tray on one hand.

"That's nothing. Police recruits are worse."

"Really?"

The waitress grimaced. "Oh, yeah. Something happens to a man when you give him a gun and a badge. The ego gets bigger and the brain gets smaller. But firemen," she grinned, "they're just hot."

Alexi smiled at the pun. Another round of laughter from the firefighters drew her attention. The men were similarly dressed in jeans and T-shirts tight enough to show off muscled chests, bulky shoulders, and ripped stomachs. The women, a minority among them, also appeared to be in prime physical condition. Theirs was a less obvious power, no bulging biceps, but instead compact bodies softened by curves in just the right places.

Alexi's thoughts drifted to Kate Chambers. Lithe and blond, Kate didn't fit Alexi's idea of a firefighter, but she had projected an air of confidence, as if daring Alexi to question her competence. Kate had made it clear she considered Alexi a suspect, and, under the scrutiny of those probing green eyes, Alexi sensed that she'd have to be careful if she had any hope of keeping her secrets.

When the front door swung open, Alexi looked up and gasped. Kate Chambers paused in the doorway, almost as if Alexi's thoughts had conjured her. She was stunning in heather gray slacks and a light blue blouse. Hair the color of corn silk floated around her face and touched her shoulders. Kate stood out in this crowd, and Alexi's wasn't the only head to turn.

Alexi had just enough time to register her irritation at herself for admiring Kate's beauty before she realized Kate was making her way toward the bar. When Kate noticed Alexi, she paused behind a stool, suddenly seeming uncertain if she wanted to sit.

"What are you doing here?" Accusation peppered Kate's words.

"I work here," Alexi snapped back.

"Here?"

"Not that it's any of your business, but I needed a job. The owner's a friend and offered to help me out." Kate's obvious displeasure annoyed Alexi. She wasn't happy about the idea of serving her either, but she didn't have much choice. She tried for a professional smile, but it felt false so she let it slide away.

Kate continued to eye her warily as she sat down.

"Do you want a drink, or what? Because I've got other customers." Alexi knew she was bordering on rudeness, but she couldn't seem to keep the edge out of her voice.

"Beer. Whatever you have on tap." Kate tried to hide her apprehension, but she hadn't seen Alexi behind the bar until it was too late. She couldn't leave now or it would seem like she was making a big deal out of what really shouldn't be.

Alexi reached under the bar for a mug. Amber liquid spilled into the glass as she pulled back the handle, and Kate watched a line of foam creep up the inside to keep from looking at Alexi's face. The discontent clearly visible on Alexi's features caused a knot of disappointment in Kate's stomach, and Kate preferred not to examine why.

A wiry man clapped a hand on Kate's shoulder as he slid onto the stool next to her and signaled for a beer. "Hey there, Barbie. I heard you got your first case."

Kate grunted an affirmative and hoped her fellow firefighter would take the hint and shut up. She wasn't supposed to meet Paula for twenty minutes, but now was rethinking her decision to have a drink at the bar while she waited. The last thing she wanted to talk about was Alexi's case.

"Got any leads?" he persisted.

Kate looked up and met Alexi's eyes as she set a bottle in front of him. Kate tried to hold her gaze, but Alexi turned away and moved down the bar to help another patron. When Kate didn't answer, the firefighter finally picked up his drink and headed for a table full of his peers.

Kate watched Alexi move smoothly behind the bar, uncapping bottles and mixing drinks. Despite her height, Alexi seemed comfortable in the confined space. With one hand she filled a glass with ice while deftly rocking a shaker with the other. She poured the drinks, then swiped her hands over the white apron encircling her hips. When she turned away to serve a new patron, Kate's eyes were drawn to the way the apron framed Alexi's firm, denim-encased ass. Alexi turned back toward her, and Kate jerked her head away so fast she thought she might have whiplash.

"Another?" Alexi paused and Kate was surprised to see a small grin. "Barbie?"

"Uh, yeah, one more."

Alexi rested her palms on the bar and leaned closer. "You're really not going to tell me?"

"It's just a stupid nickname." When Alexi waited expectantly, Kate sighed. "In the academy, one of the guys called me Firefighter Barbie."

Alexi laughed, and the sound gave Kate a rush of pleasure. It was spontaneous and genuine and less restrained than Kate would have expected from Alexi.

"That's cute." Alexi straightened and reached under the bar, bending her head to cover her widening smile. She slid another beer in front of Kate. The nickname fit. Kate resembled a life-sized version of the doll, and Alexi could easily imagine her as one of a new blue-collar professional series. Maybe she would come with her own pink fire engine.

"Cute? Ha. Makes it hard to be taken seriously." Kate took a swig from her glass. "Hell, even some of the instructors caught on and starting using it."

"So you've been proving yourself ever since?"

"I earned respect when I was on the engine. But now as an investigator I have to start all over." Kate regretted the words as soon as she said them, fearful she'd revealed too much.

"You're new at this?" Alexi was surprised by the admission. Kate projected an air of confidence and a touch of aloofness.

Kate's expression turned icy and she shoved her still-full beer away. "I've been trained well. I'm *going* to find out who set that fire."

Suddenly aware of the curious expressions of several customers seated at the bar, Alexi stuffed down a biting response. Kate had reacted quickly to the hint of a question about her competence, and Alexi could have easily let her own temper flare. But keeping cool seemed the more prudent course. "Great. Because I'm eager to put all this behind me and begin to rebuild."

Kate's eyes narrowed and Alexi could almost see her struggling with her composure as well. Finally she nodded and said, "That's good because I have some questions for you."

"Like what?"

"For starters, we checked with your alarm company and your code was used to arm the system at three thirty p.m."

"I told you that."

"It was also used to disarm it twenty minutes later."

"I don't know how that could be." Alexi and Ron each had separate access codes, as did their two shift managers.

"Does anyone else know your code?"

"Not that I know of. But couldn't someone hack into that type of system? Or is that something you see only on television?"

"We'll continue to check into it."

Alexi supposed someone could have gotten her code. But she was usually careful with sensitive information. She hadn't known any of her employees personally before she hired them. Ron and Danielle were the only two people she trusted with confidential matters. "We also have questions about your financial situation."

"My what?"

"Some of the withdrawals from the business account don't make much sense."

"I hardly think—" Alexi stopped, realizing she was raising her voice, and leaned closer so as not to be overheard. "I hardly think my finances are any of your business."

"If they had anything to do with the cause of that fire, they most certainly are."

"They didn't."

"Are you sure?"

She wasn't, but she'd be damned if she'd let Kate know that. She was aware of what difficulties had led to those withdrawals, but they were none of Kate's concern. If there was a connection, Alexi planned to find out herself before she gave any information to Kate Chambers.

"The sooner I finish my investigation, the sooner you get your insurance check. So it would behoove you to cooperate."

"Really? It would behoove me?"

"I'm serious."

"And professional, too. Accosting me at work like this."

Kate bristled at the derision in Alexi's voice. She didn't have a chance to defend herself before Alexi turned and strode to the other end of the bar to take an order. She hadn't intended to confront Alexi this way. Hell, she hadn't even known she would see Alexi tonight. But Alexi's closed-off attitude irritated her. Shouldn't Alexi be as helpful as possible? Didn't she want to know who had set the fire that destroyed her bar? Unless she already knew. What other reason would she have for stonewalling Kate, unless she was involved somehow?

"I wasn't accosting you," Kate mumbled.

"Talking to yourself, Chambers?" Paula clapped a hand on Kate's shoulder.

Kate glanced once more at Alexi, who stood with her back to Kate. "Apparently, I am."

"Well, let's get a few more drinks in you and drown out those voices." Paula hung her arm around Kate's neck and leaned forward and raised her other arm. "Yo, bartender," she shouted in Alexi's direction.

"Um, Paula." Kate made a move to grab Paula's beckoning hand. She wanted to tell her they'd get a table and order from the waitress. Clearly, Alexi didn't want to deal with her here.

She caught Paula's hand just as Alexi turned toward them. Alexi glanced between Kate and Paula, no doubt taking in the seeming embrace and their joined hands.

"Can I get you something?" Alexi's tone was detached, giving no indication Kate was anything but a customer.

Oblivious to the tension between Kate and Alexi, Paula grinned and gave Alexi a quick once-over. "Yeah, I need a beer, Sam Adams if you've got it. Kate, do you need another one?"

"No, I'm good." Kate raised the drink she'd all but abandoned. She planned on nursing that one as long as she could.

Alexi handed Paula a bottle and took the bills she dropped on the bar. Kate couldn't tell if she'd caught Paula's lingering glance. But the appraisal hadn't escaped Kate's notice, and she didn't feel like spending the night deflecting questions about whether she thought Alexi was gay.

"Let's get a table over there." She stood, leaving no chance for Paula to argue. But she waited until Paula headed for a vacant table, then she dropped her business card on the bar in front of Alexi. "Please find time to come in for a more formal conversation."

She didn't wait for a response before turning to join Paula. She hoped she'd been quick enough not to arouse Paula's suspicions. But Paula was far too observant, and Kate knew her curious expression was just the beginning.

"Did you just give the bartender your number?" Paula didn't wait for Kate to sit down.

"No." Kate set her beer on the table, then sank into her chair. "Well, yes. But it's not what you think."

"Hey, it's okay, I understand. And I'm proud of you."

"You are?"

"Yeah. You're finally going to play the field a little. Good for you." Paula lifted her bottle in a salute.

"I'm not playing the field."

"Then what?"

"She's…involved in a case I'm working."

Paula's eyes tracked to Alexi again. "That's a shame."

"Why?"

"Because she's hot. But you're too damn ethical to hook up with her if she's connected to work."

"Paula, she might be an—" the word *arsonist* never made it past her lips. "I prefer to keep my work and my personal life separate."

"You're far too practical."

Paula was all talk, and as usual, she needed Kate to point that out. "You wouldn't get involved with a patient."

"Point taken. But she's not one of my patients. Do you mind if I ask her out?"

"Yes," Kate answered much too quickly, then scrambled for a feasible explanation for her refusal. "You shouldn't get involved with her until I'm through with my case. Please."

"Okay. But once you're through she's fair game."

"Right." Kate hated the thought of Alexi as fair game. But her first priority was to determine if Alexi had anything to do with that fire. After that, she would deal with whatever else happened.

Paula nodded in Alexi's direction. "So if we're not talking about her, then where does your lust lie these days?"

Kate laughed. "I haven't dated anyone since Debbie." Kate's ex, a police officer, had accepted a position with the FBI that required relocation. When Kate hadn't been willing to leave her job, they'd taken it as a sign that they weren't meant to be. They had parted ways making empty promises to keep in touch, but beyond a few initial e-mails neither had kept that vow. If Kate was being honest, once she'd adjusted to not having someone to talk to over the dinner table, it had been relatively easy to get over Debbie leaving.

Paula paused with her beer halfway to her lips and stared at Kate. "That was almost a year ago."

"So?"

"What are you waiting for? You need to get back out there."

"I'm out there."

"So when you said you haven't dated anyone, you meant you haven't seen anyone seriously. But you've been out on dates."

"Well, no." She'd been busy. At least, that's why she told herself she hadn't had a date in nearly a year.

"Okay, we're going to fix that right now." Paula drained the rest of her beer and set the bottle on the table. She sat up straighter and began to scan the room.

"No, we're not."

"Sure, we are. There are plenty of attractive women in here. Choose one."

"This isn't a gay bar. I can't just pick one." As she glanced around, Kate forced herself to allow her gaze to linger on Alexi for only a moment. Of all of the women in the bar, including the straight ones, Alexi was the last one Kate should be looking at.

Yet, she *was* looking, and she had to pull her eyes away. Irritated, she reminded herself there was still a very good chance that Alexi was their arsonist. At the very least, Kate was certain Alexi was hiding something.

"Honey, this is a cop bar. Even when you throw in the firefighters, I'd say three-quarters of the women in here are lesbians."

"Picking up women in a bar is not my style. If it happens to me, it happens. But if not, I'm perfectly happy without a partner."

"Well, there's your problem. You're waiting for something to happen *to* you."

Kate shrugged. "It usually does eventually."

"Of course it does. Damn beautiful people," Paula grumbled with a slight smile.

"And until then I won't stress about it," Kate continued, ignoring Paula's good-natured teasing. She saw no point in correcting Paula's misconception that available women were falling at her feet. In truth, Kate knew that her introverted demeanor didn't invite advances. "Since we've established that my love life is nil, let's talk about you. Any new prospects?"

Paula shrugged. "I'm sick of dating cops and firefighters."

"I guess that lets out most of this crowd."

"Where else does one meet eligible lesbians in this town?"

"Join a softball league," Kate suggested, knowing how Paula hated the stereotype about lesbians and softball.

"Thanks."

"I don't know what else to tell you, Paula." Kate leaned forward, resting her elbows on the table in front of her.

"You really don't miss having someone around? Or get lonely at all?"

Surprised at the seriousness in Paula's tone, Kate considered the question. "Sometimes. But my situation is different. For the first few months after Debbie left, I really wasn't up for getting involved with anyone new. And then I got injured and my focus has been on getting better, then on training for this new job."

"Well, I get lonely." Paula stared at her beer, twirling the bottom of the bottle in circles on the table. "Don't look so shocked."

"I'm not. I just didn't know that you weren't happy being—"

"A slut?"

"You're not a slut." Certainly Paula was a bit freer with her affections than Kate. But then again, Paula had used the word "prude" to describe Kate on more than one occasion. Reality was little more than perception.

"Okay. But I haven't had a real relationship in a while."

"I know." In an effort to stop the rhythm of the bottle, Kate lifted it from Paula's hand and set it aside. "But you've had—ah—interactions. And I didn't know you weren't satisfied with that type of relationship."

"Well, I've been very satisfied at times," Paula said with a grin. "But I'm not getting any younger here. I'd like to have someone to organize my meds when I get too old to remember when I take the little red pill."

Kate laughed. "You could hire a hot young nurse to do that."

"Hmm, I hadn't thought of that."

"Problem solved."

Paula's expression suddenly turned more serious than Kate had ever seen it. "I might want to have kids."

Kate paused with her glass resting against her lower lip. Seconds later and she would have choked on a mouthful of beer. "You…you want—"

"Come on. Is that so hard to believe? I'm not some cold, emotionless—"

"I know, I know. But you've never talked about any of this before. Why now?"

"God, I don't know," Paula growled, shoving a hand into her hair. "I never thought I would be one of those people that freaked out about getting older, but I'm turning forty next month."

"Ah, it's all making sense now. This is a mid-life crisis."

"Keep joking. You're not that far from forty yourself."

"Hey, now. I haven't passed thirty-five yet."

"Give me back my beer."

Kate slid the bottle across the table. "All right, so you want to get married and have kids."

"I don't know about married, but…yeah, maybe."

"Wow. I need to take this in."

"Well, don't think about it too hard. I'm not making any sudden moves. It's just something that's been on my mind lately."

"Whatever makes you happy, babe." Kate raised her glass and tapped it against Paula's bottle. She couldn't say she hadn't thought about the future from time to time. Would she meet someone with whom she could talk about forever? Did she want a family? Maybe. But she'd been cruising through life feeling as if she were still in her twenties, and those serious issues always seemed to be something she would deal with *someday.* Could someday be sooner than she'd thought?

Chapter Five

Alexi parked the Cadillac on the street in front of In Left Field and stepped out. A slight breeze stirred the humid night air around her and carried the sharp scent of smoke. Overhead, the streetlight buzzed and flickered then went off, leaving Alexi in darkness. She squinted at her bar through the sting of tears. She didn't remember leaving a light on inside when she closed up. But as she looked closer, she knew the orange glow wasn't lamplight.

She rushed to the front door and pulled, but it wouldn't open. As she fumbled through her pockets, fear pulsed through her veins. Where were her keys? She always kept them in her pocket, but they weren't there. She shoved her hands in the pocket of her overcoat and again came up empty. Her throat burned, dry and hot, as she inhaled the smoke rolling from beneath the front door. Desperately, she yanked on the handle, but it wouldn't budge.

A loud banging came from the back of the building. Alexi rounded the corner and headed toward the noise. At the other end of the alley, a figure dressed in black moved in the shadows of the doorway.

"Hey, what are you doing back here?" Alexi called.

When the figure took off, Alexi tried to run after him, but she seemed to be going in slow motion. She churned her legs and pumped her arms but it was as if she was trying to run underwater. The man increased the distance between them with every step as they twisted and turned through the alleys and onto the empty street a block away from the bar.

Alexi stumbled to a stop on Demonbruen Street in front of the Country Music Hall of Fame. Now nearly two blocks away, the man cut up Sixth Avenue behind the Sommet Center and was out of sight in seconds.

The sound of approaching sirens pulled her attention back to the bar. After one last look in the direction in which the man disappeared, Alexi turned away. She rounded the corner as a fire engine pulled up to the curb. Four men in turnout gear tumbled out of the cab and immediately went to work. By now thick smoke poured from the building and flames danced inside the windows. As Alexi ran back through the alley, she heard the sound of glass breaking under the heat of the fire. Two firefighters stretched a hose toward the front of the building while a third attached the end of the hose to a panel on the side of the vehicle. He immediately began to flip switches and check gauges.

"I chased a guy—by the arena," Alexi yelled between panting breaths as she rushed up to the fire engine and grabbed the sleeve of the nearest man.

"The police will be here soon and you can give them a description." The firefighter tried to shake off her hand, but Alexi clung to the heavy material of the coat.

"But I didn't see his face," Alexi said desperately.

"Ma'am, you need to stand back and let us do our jobs."

A solid crack sounded from behind her, and Alexi whipped her head around in time to see firefighters rush through the now-broken front door. Dark smoke poured out and, freed from the confines of the building, it curled into the night sky.

"Oh, my God, you've got to save my bar." Panic brought a shrill edge to Alexi's voice and she began to tremble.

The firefighter grabbed Alexi's upper arms, steadying her. "Ma'am, you have to give us room to work."

Something in the firm, even alto broke through the fear and

Alexi released her grip on the firefighter's coat. She looked up and was shocked to find clear green eyes behind the firefighter's shield.

"Kate?" she whispered.

Confusion clouded Kate's eyes but her voice remained resolute. "Stay here."

Before Alexi could respond, Kate released her and ran toward the building. She disappeared into the inferno, swallowed up by smoke and flames.

Alexi awoke with fear still driving her heart rate and the image of Kate's eyes lingering in her head. She rolled to her back and pulled the twisted sheet from around her legs, apparently having kicked off the rest of the covers in the night. Above her, the ceiling fan spun and a breeze feathered over Alexi's warm skin.

She rubbed a hand across her forehead and tried to hold onto the fragile threads of the dream. The figure in black had clearly been a creation of her imagination and she'd assumed it was a man. But the suspect's build hadn't been obviously masculine or feminine, and now she struggled to remember if she had noticed any clues in the stride or carriage as the mysterious person ran away. Frustrated when she couldn't recall anything that might provide a hint, she reminded herself that even if she could, the details would be of her dream and not necessarily the real arsonist.

And Kate was not real either, at least not the dream version, but she couldn't shake the image of those steady, green eyes or the assurance in Kate's voice. She experienced the same twinge in her chest as she had in the dream when she remembered discovering Kate behind the firefighter's mask. It was no surprise that Kate had made an appearance. It wasn't even difficult to determine how she'd come to end up behind the mask. The night before, Alexi had Googled Kate and read about her injury while she was assigned to an engine company. The most current newspaper article she could find stated that Kate had regained consciousness and was expected to make a full recovery. But obviously something had necessitated a move to the fire marshal's office, and Alexi had gotten the impression that Kate hadn't volunteered for the change.

What Alexi hadn't anticipated was the calming effect of Dream-Kate as a firefighter, when, in real life, the investigator stirred antagonistic unease in Alexi.

"I'm on my way in, Jason." Kate stood on one leg in the middle of her bedroom, trying to balance her cell between her ear and shoulder and pull her pants on at the same time. "No, that's okay. You drop the kids off at school and I'll meet you at the office."

She flipped the phone closed and shoved it in her pocket. In what had become a new routine, Kate pinned a badge and nameplate onto a starched and pressed white polyester-blend shirt, then shrugged it on. As she walked down the hallway to the living room, she tucked her shirt into her dark navy slacks. Her stiff leather belt was draped over the back of the sofa where she'd left it after she took it off the night before. She hated this new uniform and doubted she'd ever stop missing the comfortable T-shirts and BDU pants that were commonplace around the fire station. Once in a while she found herself longing for the weight of a turnout jacket and SCBA tank. She would even take her turn mopping the truck bay without grumbling if it would get her back on an engine.

She scooped up her keys and headed out the front door, patting her pockets to make sure she hadn't forgotten anything. In the parking lot, she climbed into the Tahoe, the one perk to her new job—less money spent on gas. Still not a fair trade-off, but after being chastised by Paula she was trying to be more positive.

As she drove, she mentally reviewed her schedule for the day. Unless they got a new case, she would spend the entire time working on the In Left Field arson. The results should begin coming back from the lab today. Kate knew they would confirm that an accelerant was used, but she didn't think they would discover much more. They'd probably make more headway following the financial leads from the day before. She prepared herself for the possibility that the evidence would continue to point to Alexi, and maybe her partner, Ron.

They had several employees of the bar left to track down and interview. And Ron Volk was scheduled to come in to the office and meet with Kate and Jason later this morning. Kate planned to call Ron's wife and ask her to accompany him. After Kate's encounter with Alexi the night before, she would be surprised if she heard from Alexi today. Kate hadn't exactly *accosted* her, as Alexi had accused, but perhaps she could have handled things a bit more discreetly. She'd been caught off guard at seeing Alexi behind the bar at the Blue Line.

Kate didn't necessarily consider herself a regular at the bar, but she did go there when she needed to unwind. She found comfort among her peers—firefighters and police officers—people who knew the stresses of their job. Oftentimes, it was difficult for the civilians in their lives to understand how their job affected them. Luckily, with the exception of her mother, Kate's family got it. Her father was a career engineer at Station 32, and her older brother had followed easily in his footsteps, although he'd found his place on a rescue truck wielding heavy extrication tools. Kate's path to firefighting had been met with a little more resistance. As a child, Kate's mother had curled her pale blond hair into ringlets and put her in frilly dresses. Later, she'd been steered toward cheerleading and dating. The pleated skirt and tight sweater had fit fine, but she'd never been comfortable with the boys.

She knew her mother always hoped she'd grow out of wanting to be a firefighter. One night at dinner, two weeks before her college graduation, Kate announced that she'd applied to the fire academy, and across the table her mother's disappointment was palpable. The only time Kate had seen her mother more disappointed was when Kate told her she was a lesbian. *I guess she's probably thrilled now that I'm behind a desk for the rest of my career. If only I would meet a nice young man.* Kate grimaced. Her mother didn't deserve her bitterness. While her mother didn't always approve of Kate's choices, she'd never wished Kate anything but success.

Kate's father had been the supportive parent Kate had needed. He had immediately begun to quiz her every night at the dinner table. Before she even started in the academy she had a thorough knowledge of fire behavior and could quote the water-flow rates for every type of hose diameter the Nashville department used. Kate's brother handled her physical training. He woke her early four mornings a week for a five-mile run, and when they returned to the house they lifted weights in the garage until her arms felt like rubber. She dragged the dummy he borrowed from the academy up and down ladders and through the house. For weeks, from the moment she got home in the afternoon until she went to bed at night, she carried that dummy everywhere with her.

As Kate steered the Tahoe into the office parking lot, she shoved aside thoughts of her family. Back to business. She needed to organize her theories about the investigation. Her head felt like it was going in three different directions, and she hoped that was only because this was her first case.

Alexi stared at the business card Kate Chambers had so arrogantly thrown on the bar the night before. Now it rested harmlessly on the coffee table in front of her. Considering the lingering sensation of this morning's dream, Alexi did not look forward to making this phone call. She leaned forward and brushed her fingers over the card, as if she could determine something about Kate from the raised font on the card. But she left it lying there and picked up the coffee mug next to it instead.

She could put off the call until tomorrow. But Kate knew where to find her and might just show up at the Blue Line again tonight. Besides, she reminded herself, she would only delay the inevitable. Surely, Kate would soon realize that Alexi had nothing to do with the fire; then she and Kate would be on the same side. They both wanted to finish the investigation, Kate to close her case and Alexi to rebuild her business. Kate held all the cards, and that was perhaps one of the things that annoyed Alexi. Her life was in a holding pattern and would remain so until Kate was satisfied. So, with a deep breath, she decided it was time to stop fearing what Kate might find and make the call.

She picked up her cell phone and dialed, then ended the connection quickly. Maybe she *would* wait until tomorrow. Certainly anything she could tell Kate about the fire would keep until then. Yes, tomorrow—or maybe the next day.

She'd taken three steps toward the kitchen when her phone rang. She answered it without thinking.

"Ms. Clark? It's Kate Chambers. Did you call me?"

"Shit," Alexi muttered.

"What?"

"Um—nothing." *Damn caller ID.* "Sorry, I must have lost my signal. You asked me to call."

"My morning is jammed." Alexi could hear shuffling papers through the phone and Kate sounded distracted. "Can you come in this afternoon?"

"Come in? To your office?" Suddenly, Alexi's stomach was a bundle of nerves. She was innocent and this was a chance to convince Kate of that fact. But just hearing Kate's smooth, professional voice had her knotted up.

"Yes. We need to go over a few things."

"Could we meet someplace else?" Perhaps neutral ground would help Alexi regain her composure.

"What did you have in mind?"

"How about that coffee shop across the street from my bar?"

There was a long pause, but Alexi waited Kate out.

"Okay. One o'clock," Kate finally agreed.

"See you then," Alexi said before she snapped the phone shut. She exhaled slowly. "Coffee. I need coffee."

Alexi hurried to the kitchen and poured a fresh cup from the carafe. She took a sip and sighed. She'd picked up her coffee habit only after she stopped drinking. But she didn't stress about trading one addiction for another, deciding as long as she didn't join the crowd huddled by the back door to smoke after AA meetings she was still ahead of the game.

Memories of her father, weak, ashen, and wracked with the pain of lung cancer kept her from lighting up. Diagnosed in his late forties, he'd died barely nine months later, when Alexi was twenty-four years old. Alexi was devastated, and alcohol was the only thing that seemed to ease her pain. In the months following his death, Alexi had shut down, eventually driving away the woman she'd been dating since high school. An already strained relationship with her mother grew more so, precisely at the time when they should have been coming together in their shared misery. She'd blamed her mother for allowing him to smoke all those years, even while she drank enough to destroy her own body. And Alexi suspected on some level her mother was relieved to see her pull away, because she didn't want to watch Alexi kill herself. So they both embraced anger instead of fear and sadness.

After many years and several failed attempts at sobriety, Alexi could now admit that her grief had not only compounded her denial but also provided her friends with an excuse not to confront her about her drinking. They rationalized her problem just as she did, and they all seemed to believe that she would stop drinking after she'd dealt with her father's death. But that day hadn't come, and Alexi had only continued to push them away until only Danielle was left.

She slid so seamlessly from social drinking into a serious habit that she couldn't even pinpoint the moment when she lost her grip. Working toward owning her bar was the one thing that gave her the shred of strength to stay semi-functional. A tumbler of vodka tucked under the bar kept her hands from shaking but, when sipped slowly, wasn't enough to make it impossible for her to work. And if her co-workers noticed, they turned a blind eye as well.

Later, alone in her apartment, while she chased the elusive thread of sleep, she often drank until she passed out. She could stave off stress, both emotional and environmental, for as long as she kept the glass full. She hurt all the time, but at least she could control when she faced those demons. And she chose to do so alone, trembling in her darkened apartment.

Alexi shook her head, shoving aside old ghosts, and finished the end of her coffee. This wasn't the time to lament her miserable past. She'd done what she could to make amends to others, and she'd just have to live with the scars she'd inflicted on herself.

CHAPTER SIX

Alexi stepped out of the shower to the sound of her doorbell. On her way through the bedroom, she grabbed her robe and slipped it on. She checked the peephole then opened the door.

"Coffee made?" Ron asked as he walked in and headed directly toward the kitchen.

"Good morning to you, too." Alexi moved aside and waited for Danielle to come in.

"Sorry," Danielle muttered.

"Don't worry about it."

Alexi entered the kitchen in time to see Ron pouring a full mug of coffee into the sink. Jack wound between Ron's ankles, but Ron ignored him.

"It's cold."

"I wasn't expecting guests. What's up?"

When Alexi made no move to brew fresh coffee, Danielle reached around Ron for the carafe and began to make it.

"We're on our way downtown to meet with the arson investigators." Ron strode across the kitchen then back to stand near the sink. "I wish they would just finish whatever they need to."

"I know. I have to meet with them this afternoon." Alexi braced a hip against the counter.

"What are you going to say?"

Ron's voice carried a hint of accusation and Alexi tried not to be annoyed. Ron was under the same stress she was, and they simply had different ways of dealing with it.

"The truth. For what it's worth. I don't know any more than you do. I closed up, and the next thing I knew I woke up to the phone ringing and news of the fire."

"So what are we going to do now?"

"We're going to rebuild as soon as the insurance company pays up."

Ron shook his head slowly. "It's a lot of work."

"What are you saying, Ron?" Alexi stopped and stared at him. She'd assumed they were all of the same mind regarding their future.

"Maybe it's time to consider cutting our losses."

"Cutting our losses?" Alexi glanced at Danielle, who kept her back to Alexi and continued prepping the coffeemaker. "Cutting our losses?" Alexi repeated. If she said it again, only louder, it might make things more clear.

Ron held up his hands and smiled stiffly. "Yeah. We had a good run. But maybe now is the time to go our separate ways, in business anyway."

"We had a good...go our separate...I can't believe I'm hearing this." Alexi pressed her palms to the countertop, imagining that the cool granite could somehow douse her rising anger. She wouldn't give up her bar without a fight, and she wasn't afraid to take the offensive. "Let's talk about our losses, Ron."

"What do you mean?"

"I think you know exactly what I mean. Why does Kate Chambers want to ask me about our financial records?"

"I don't know," he said, but the panic that flashed in his eyes told a different story. "Who knows what those investigators will try to pin on us. They're probably working with the insurance company so they won't have to pay. You read about this stuff all the time."

Alexi would have laughed at the ridiculousness of his

suggestion if he didn't look so nervous. His eyes darted away from hers to Danielle, and perspiration dotted his forehead.

"So when I meet with her this afternoon and she shows me our bank statements, what am I going to see?" Alexi asked the question she already knew the answer to—the question that had a sick feeling churning in her stomach. She'd been turning her back on the money situation for months, telling herself if she ignored the issue it would go away. Once again, Alexi had allowed fear to push her to denial. For all the progress she'd thought she'd made in the past year, she was really no better at solving her problems.

Ron didn't answer. But, as if on cue, Danielle turned and put an arm around Alexi's shoulders.

"Don't you remember what it was like when we first started out? Honey, the insurance company is only going to give us what the property was worth. We'd still have to do all of the work to rebuild and reopen. We're just saying that might not be our best option."

"We? So you agree with this?"

Danielle's eyes cut to Ron.

Alexi pulled away from Danielle. "Don't look at him. Answer me."

Ron jumped in. "Have you forgotten the long hours we put in during the first few years?"

"We've already got a staff and loyal customers and—" Alexi shook her head, confused about why they were having this argument. She couldn't believe they were even discussing not rebuilding the bar. "Danielle, seriously, you're on board with this idea?"

Ron didn't give Danielle time to answer. "We're in agree—"

"Danielle?"

Danielle stared at the tile floor. "Yes. Completely."

"Look at me."

"We're not as young as we were last time." Danielle's eyes

remained downcast, and Alexi suspected Danielle couldn't bring herself to look her in the eye when she lied to her. "Ron and I want to have kids. We need more stability."

"I see." Alexi knew how badly Danielle wanted children, and over the years she'd gotten the impression that Ron didn't, despite what he'd apparently told Danielle.

Now for some reason Ron wanted out, and he was using the lure of starting a family to get Danielle in his corner. Alexi wasn't surprised that he would see the promise of an insurance payout as an opportunity to split. She'd known that the day-to-day operation of the bar was wearing on Ron. Ultimately, he wanted to be a hands-off investor, sitting back and collecting his profits, but he couldn't trust anyone enough not to micromanage things. Did he want out badly enough to commit arson?

"What are you afraid of, Ron?"

Ron glanced at Danielle, then back at Alexi. "Nothing. Danielle and I are just at a different place now than you are. This decision is easier for you because you don't have a life outside the bar."

Alexi flinched. "Real nice, Ron."

"He didn't mean—"

Alexi shrugged Danielle's arm off her shoulder. "Yes, he did. It's okay. He's not wrong."

"Alexi—"

"Listen, I've got some errands to run. And you should get going. You don't want to be late for your appointment with the investigators."

"They can damn well wait until I've had my coffee."

Alexi removed the carafe and stuck a travel mug under the stream of coffee.

"Here. Drink it on the way." Without waiting for an answer she pressed the mug into his hand.

"We're not done talking about the bar."

"Yes we are, for now anyway." With a hand on Danielle's shoulder, Alexi steered them both toward the door. They hadn't resolved the question of their future, but Alexi just wanted them out of her apartment. They didn't have to make any immediate decisions regarding the bar until Chambers and her partner completed their report anyway. Today, Alexi's focus needed to be on her afternoon meeting with Chambers, then later she'd face the inevitable confrontation with Ron.

❖

"Mrs. Volk, you're in here. Mr. Volk, if you would, come with me." Jason showed Danielle Volk into the conference room. Kate, already seated on one side of the table, stood to greet her.

"I thought we would be speaking with you together," Ron protested. When he took a step toward the conference room, Jason moved to block his entrance.

"Actually, things will go much more quickly this way. We'll just be in the next room."

Before he could argue any further, Jason closed the door to the conference room, leaving Kate alone with Danielle.

"Please, have a seat, Mrs. Volk." Kate gestured across the table from her.

Danielle's hand trembled as she pulled out the chair. Kate waited until Danielle was seated, then she flipped the notebook in front of her to a page of notes she'd taken earlier and clicked her pen.

"Mrs. Volk, your husband stated that he was with you the night of the fire."

Danielle cleared her throat. "That's right. He came home from the bar early."

"Then what did you do?"

"We talked for a while and went to bed."

"What time was that?"

"About two a.m."

"Is there any chance he left the house after you were asleep?"

"No," Danielle answered quickly.

"Are you sure?"

"I'm a light sleeper."

Kate didn't speak for a long moment. She pretended to consult her notes, even though she already knew what she wanted to ask. People often talked to fill an uncomfortable silence, and those were sometimes the most telling statements. But, though Danielle fidgeted in her chair, she didn't say a word.

"And what about Ms. Clark? Do you know where she was that night?" Kate failed to block out the image of Alexi's face as she asked the question.

"She said she went home after closing up."

Kate considered her next statement carefully. She was certain Danielle was hiding something and she wasn't likely to spill it when her husband was around.

"Mrs. Volk—" Kate leaned forward and rested her forearms on the table. She glanced at the door, on the other side of which Jason was having a similar conversation with Ron Volk—"we've determined the fire was the result of arson. If you know anything that could help us find who did this, it's best if you tell us now. Even if you weren't involved, if I find out later that you concealed something from us, things could go very badly for you."

Danielle met Kate's eyes and her demeanor changed immediately. Her jaw tightened and her expression hardened. "Neither my husband or Alexi had anything to do with that fire." Her eyes flashed fiercely and Kate reassessed her opinion of Danielle Volk. She wasn't the meek creature Kate had originally thought. When challenged she was as protective as a mother lion.

❖

Kate parked the Tahoe on the street in front of Alexi's bar. The building's remains were just as they had been the night of the fire. Daylight brought home the devastation Alexi and her partner faced. Kate wondered if they had been able to salvage anything from inside.

She had just turned toward the coffee shop across the street when a noise from the alley caught her attention and she headed that way instead. Alexi's Cadillac was parked beside the bar, and Kate skirted it as she continued toward the old carriage house at the end of the alley.

Inside the open doors, Alexi leaned under the hood of a vintage Chevelle. A halogen work light hung on the inside of the hood and cast a white glow over the engine.

The night of the fire, Kate had noticed the carriage house and had determined it was locked and not tampered with. When she'd mentioned it to Jason, he said he'd asked Ron Volk for a key and Mr. Volk refused. Since the garage was unaffected by the fire, they'd need to involve the police and get a warrant to search it. Jason didn't believe they had cause to ask for a warrant, but Kate had kept the building in the back of her mind. Maybe now she'd get a good-enough look around the interior of the garage to determine if it was worth convincing Jason to get that warrant. A few minutes of conversation to distract Alexi could save her hours of legwork.

Alexi rested her weight on one hand as she stretched to reach farther under the hood. She bent a leg to tap her toe against the floor to balance herself, and the muscles of her arm strained against the sleeve of her T-shirt as she pulled on a socket wrench. When the bolt didn't budge she growled, a low sound of frustration that Kate found extremely sexy. She grunted softly and tugged harder on the wrench handle.

Shoving aside her inappropriate thoughts, Kate cleared her throat and said, "Nice car." Fire Engine Red paint shone under the fluorescent overhead light. She glanced at the sleek black machine parked outside in the alley. "Quite a departure from the Caddy."

Alexi straightened and rested a hip against the front quarter-panel. "A girl needs some variety, doesn't she?"

When Alexi smiled at her like that, Kate could forget that she was supposed to be casing the garage. She moved close enough to trace her hand over the curve of the car's roof. "Well, you've definitely got that here." The refined, graceful style of the Cadillac varied greatly from the obvious power of the Chevelle. And though she hardly knew Alexi, she thought the Caddy might be a better fit. She suspected the Cadillac had plenty of aggression beneath the hood, but it was cloaked by the understated exterior.

"The Chevelle was my dad's car."

"Nice." Kate leaned down to look in the open driver's window. The outside was pristine but the inside still needed work. The vinyl seats were worn and cracked in places. The dials in the dash looked original, as did the radio, and Kate wondered if it still worked.

"He was fixing it up when—" Alexi placed the wrench on a nearby workbench, picked up a rag, and wiped her hands. "It's been sitting in this garage under a tarp for too long. I think I'm in over my head trying to get it running again now."

"Nah, like most things in life, it just needs some time and patience." Kate tapped a hand on the edge of the window frame and straightened.

"The last thing I need right now is philosophy from you, Ms. Chambers."

Kate blinked. She'd let the spark between them go to her head, and now the distance in Alexi's voice stung. But they didn't know each other, and their interaction was *supposed* to be professional. There was no reason they should have any warmth between them.

"I'm sorry." Kate stepped away from the car, and as she turned she scanned the shelves over the workbench. "I was a little early and I heard you down here so—well, I'll wait for you in the coffee shop." As her gaze swept lower she spotted a gas can under the bench. Could she have just found their accelerant?

"Take it." Kate whipped her head around and found Alexi's eyes on her. Alexi flicked a glance at the gas can and then back. "Take it. But I'll tell you now, you'll find my prints on it."

"What about Mr. Volk?"

"I don't think so. He doesn't use the garage."

Kate pulled an evidence bag from her jacket pocket and wrapped it around the handle of the gas can before she picked it up. "Does he have a key?"

"Yes."

"Who else?"

"Just he and I." Alexi sighed and slammed the hood on the Chevelle. "Are you hungry?"

"I could eat." By the time Kate had finished with Danielle Volk, she'd had just enough time to write up her notes and confer with Jason about his interview before heading out to meet Alexi.

"They've got great sandwiches across the street." Alexi stepped outside the garage, and after Kate followed, she pulled the doors closed and snapped the padlock closed. Alexi stared at the charred shell of her bar. Seeing the misery in her eyes, Kate couldn't imagine that she was the one to inflict such damage. Clearly, the bar was more than just real estate, or even a business to Alexi.

"One of the first guys on scene told me they were afraid the garage would go up too. We had an engine crew back here throwing water on the south wall."

"I don't know what I would have done if I'd lost my father's car. It's bad enough that half the memorabilia in the bar was his."

"Is he pissed?" Kate asked.

"He passed away almost fifteen years ago." Alexi turned away quickly and headed up the alley toward the street.

"I'm sorry. I didn't know." Kate caught up with Alexi at the mouth of the alley and fell into step beside her.

"I'm surprised you haven't had me thoroughly investigated."

"Just what's relevant to the business." Kate hated that Alexi thought she'd been prying into her life, even though, to an extent, she had. She stowed the gas can in her Tahoe, then they crossed the street.

Kate pulled open the door to the coffee shop. "I really am sorry to hear about your dad."

"It was a long time ago." Alexi's shoulder brushed Kate's chest as she passed.

"Yeah, but," Kate touched Alexi's arm and Alexi stopped in the doorway, "losing those reminders of him must feel like losing a part of him again. And for that, I'm sorry."

Alexi stared at Kate, astonished at how accurately Kate had read her feelings. She'd expected accusations, but sympathy and understanding were a surprise. She was jolted out of the moment when she heard a throat being cleared. A well-dressed older man stood waiting to leave and Alexi still blocked the door.

"I'm sorry," she mumbled as she moved aside, but he grumbled impatiently as he hurried past her.

"Let's sit over here." Kate guided Alexi to a table near the front window, away from the rest of the shop's occupants. "What can I get you?"

"Coffee, black, and turkey on rye."

Alexi waited while Kate went to the counter and placed their orders. Kate leaned against the counter and chatted with the friendly barista. The woman's smile was quick and wide, and she was obviously captivated by Kate. And why not? Kate's long, lean body cut an impressive figure in the sharply pressed uniform with the gleaming badge and nameplate. And something about her golden hair smoothed neatly into a bun made Alexi want to see how it would look tumbling over her shoulders. Yes, she was attractive. But she was also trying to prove that Alexi was an arsonist, and Alexi would do well to remember that.

Kate returned and set a covered cup and a wrapped sandwich in front of Alexi. "Man, have you ever tried to order black coffee in a place like this? Everything is a venti-mocha, half-caf something or other."

Alexi started to smile, then pulled it back. She recalled Kate blindsiding her about her financial matters at the bar the night before and was reminded that they weren't here for small talk.

"You had something to ask me?"

Kate paused, then opened her notebook. "Yes. There have been some questionable withdrawals from your business account."

"Questionable?" Alexi knew exactly which transactions Kate referred to. For too long, she'd trusted Ron completely when it came to the books. She had her hands full with the day-to-day operations, and honestly, she enjoyed the hands-on part of the business so much more. But she'd been livid when she discovered Ron had been pulling money from their account without her knowledge. Just three weeks before the fire, they'd had an argument about it and he had promised it wouldn't happen again.

"I've highlighted the dates and amounts." Kate slid a piece of paper in front of Alexi.

Alexi could feel Kate watching for her reaction as she scanned the figures. She carefully masked her surprise at the unexpected withdrawal four days ago.

"Can you explain these?" Kate pressed.

Alexi met Kate's eyes. "Business expenses."

Kate glanced down at the sheet, then back at Alexi. "You have this much expense in a month?"

"Yes." Alexi didn't flinch under Kate's unwavering stare. If Kate was trying to intimidate her, she was out of her league. Alexi was an accomplished liar going back to the times when she hid her liquor bottles from her ex-girlfriend. A trait she wasn't necessarily proud of but one that was useful nonetheless.

"Do you have receipts?"

"Do I need them?" Alexi pushed the paper back across the table. "Are you checking my tax return or investigating arson?"

"Ms. Clark, I had hoped you might cooperate—"

"If you *hoped* I would help you prove I burned my own bar down, you were mistaken."

Kate sighed and tucked the sheet back inside a manila folder. First she'd been stonewalled by Danielle Volk and now Alexi Clark. These women certainly knew how to circle the wagons. "I'm trying to get to the truth."

"I had nothing to do with this fire and that's the truth."

Kate wanted to believe her. She had been following each new thread of the case with the hope that they would lead away from Alexi. But if it turned out that Alexi did have something to do with the fire, there was nothing Kate could to do protect her. Kate had a job to do and she didn't intend to screw it up on her very first case.

Chapter Seven

High-rise buildings grew out of the center of downtown as Kate followed the flowing lines of the interstate toward the city. She checked her mirror and changed lanes, anticipating her exit. Having grown up here, Kate had watched the skyline change and spread outward over the years. It seemed as if every six months, a large crane erected a new building, taller than the last. But somehow, Nashville retained the feel of a small town within the big city.

She passed the football stadium, then crossed the bridge over the Cumberland River. She'd once responded to a man who had jumped off this same bridge. They had scoured the shoreline and divers had searched until dark with no luck. The next morning, his body was found fifty yards downstream. In her time riding an engine, she'd seen a wide variety of emergencies, both fire and medical in nature. She had been invincible and strong as she carried victims from the flames and had shed her tears when, despite all of her effort, a soul was lost. While her motivation to save lives and property and make her community a better place was certainly altruistic, Kate also thrived on the power of fighting one of nature's strongest elements. She enjoyed the rush of staring down a wall of flames and feeling the heat even through layers of protective gear.

It's amazing how life can change in the span of a year, she thought as she turned onto Third Avenue. Now, she was on her way back to her office with her notes from her meeting with Alexi. She would spend her shift sitting behind a desk rather than racing toward a call. She parked in front of the office, grabbed her notebook and the gas can, and headed inside.

"Did you get anywhere with Ms. Clark?" Jason asked when she walked in.

"No. But I'm certain there's something she isn't telling us." Kate crossed to her desk and booted up her desktop computer. "On a positive note, I got a look inside that garage. Both owners have keys to it, but Ms. Clark is the one who primarily uses it. She gave me permission to take the gas can."

"Check it for prints. But if theirs are the only ones on it, we won't be able to do much with it. Having gasoline in a garage isn't exactly a smoking gun."

Kate mentally reviewed their progress. Alexi's alarm code was used to disarm the system, her prints were probably on the gas can, but given that she was the owner, that wasn't definitive. They hadn't been able to pull any prints off the concrete that was planted inside. And statements from the witness and other employees hadn't sent up any red flags.

"We're not making much headway on this case, are we?" Kate dropped into her chair with a heavy sigh.

"Every case is different. Sometimes we have a ton of leads, and other times it's more about trying to make something out of very little evidence."

"You really like this, don't you?" Kate had assumed that the other investigators also had taken the assignment to avoid a worse fate. But Jason seemed genuinely committed to his work.

"Yeah, I do. It's like a puzzle. Some of the pieces are scientific and logical, but when you throw in the human element, the solution becomes complex and much more interesting."

"Okay, but don't you miss riding an engine?" When Kate

first joined the department, Jason had been on Engine 13 and the Hazmat team.

"Sure, sometimes."

"What do we do if nothing breaks?" Kate opened her notebook to review her notes, searching for something they'd missed.

"Eventually, if we don't get anywhere, we'll file it as arson by an unknown suspect."

"We just give up?"

Jason shrugged. "We can't win them all."

"Come on, Jason. You've got to do better than that. Otherwise, what's the point of our job?" Kate threw her pen down on the desk in frustration.

"We don't have infinite time for every case. There comes a point when we have to file our report based on the evidence in front of us. Then it's up to the property owner and the insurance company to fight it out."

"That's not good enough."

"Someday it will be."

Kate waited for him to elaborate, but he turned his attention back to his computer screen. Sighing, Kate picked up her pen and followed suit. She doubted she would change her opinion about her new job anytime soon.

"Do you work every day?" Ron asked from the doorway of the nearly empty Blue Line bar.

"Edna's kid is sick." Alexi finished wiping a table, then turned around. It was just shy of four o'clock and the evening crowd hadn't begun coming in yet. The sole waitress was on a smoke break behind the building and Alexi was covering the bar as well as the tables.

"Doesn't it bother you to slave away in someone else's

place?" Ron wandered inside and toward the bar. "Let me have a scotch and soda, will you?"

"I can't exactly work in ours right now. This keeps me busy." Alexi rounded the bar and poured his drink.

"I couldn't do it."

"No," Alexi murmured. "You'd rather let someone else work to pay your debts."

"What is that supposed to mean?"

"I don't know. Could it have anything to do with the two men in cheap suits who came into the bar looking for you last week?" As owner of a sports bar, Alexi was used to seeing broad-shouldered, thick-necked former football players, but these two were different. From their ill-fitting suits to their cheap shoes, they had stood out from the moment they entered. They'd made a bee-line for the bar and asked for Ron, then left immediately after Alexi told them he wasn't working that night. And when she'd asked Ron about it the next day, he'd blown her off, saying they were "business associates," but they both knew she saw through his words. Alexi laughed bitterly. "You didn't even pretend you didn't know who they were?"

"There was no point. I told you I would handle it." He shrugged and sipped his drink.

"You also told me you wouldn't take any more money." Three months ago, when she'd first discovered the funds missing from their business account, she had been livid. Accustomed to Ron being the steady, reliable one in their partnership, she'd believed him when he promised it wouldn't happen again. But it had, several times, and Alexi's patience was wearing thin. She hadn't worked so hard to put profit in the bank just so he could gamble it all away.

"Alexi, you don't understand. These guys are serious. I needed something to hold them off."

"You should have come to me."

"Why? So I could get another lecture about how hard *you*

work to keep the bar in the black. You know, I'm not so sure I like the new high-and-mighty you."

"I thought you were done gambling." Alexi ignored the barb. They wouldn't get anywhere by trading insults.

The last time Alexi found money missing, she confronted Ron. He swore it wouldn't happen again and asked her not to tell Danielle. She hated keeping things from her friend but told herself it was for the good of the business as well as Ron and Danielle's marriage.

"If LSU had just covered the spread against Alabama, I would've had enough to get square."

"And then what?" Alexi didn't believe for a minute that Ron would have stopped gambling once he was out of debt. "I can't…" Alexi stopped and took a deep breath. "You have a problem and you need to get help."

"Where do you get off accusing me? Danielle and I stood by you for years when you couldn't even get through a shift without a drink. You can't even give me a break for a few months?"

"I never once took anything from the business." Familiar guilt flooded Alexi and she wondered if she owed him a little more slack. She shook her head. She owned her mistakes, but they weren't excuse enough for Ron's current behavior. "You know I appreciate how much you both supported me. That's why I want to help you avoid going through the same thing."

"This is different. I'm not an addict. I'm just making a few bets."

"Thugs don't visit you over a few bets."

"Alexi—"

"No." Alexi couldn't stomach one more attempt to justify their current situation. "You're taking money from our business account to pay off your bookie. And now I have to figure out how to explain that to the woman who is investigating the fire that destroyed our bar."

"What did you tell the investigator?"

"Jesus, Ron, I'm talking about everything we've worked for here."

"So am I. You didn't tell her why I took the money, did you?" He slid his glass across the bar and gestured for a refill.

Irritated, Alexi took the glass and shoved it in the sink under the bar, taking petty pleasure in denying him. "No, I didn't." When a group of men came in and gathered at the other end of the bar, Alexi lowered her voice. "She thinks I set that fire. We could lose the insurance money. Hell, I could go to jail. Could things get any worse?"

He waved a hand dismissively. "Don't be ridiculous. You didn't start that fire."

"Of course not. But she thinks I did."

"Well, she doesn't have any proof. So what she *thinks* doesn't really matter, does it?"

Alexi sighed and turned away to take care of the new customers. She took their order and automatically made their drinks, all the while considering Ron's words. Why did she care? Why did Kate Chambers's opinion matter? It didn't. It shouldn't. Time would prove Alexi's innocence, and beyond that, she had no reason to be thinking about Kate.

But she was. She was remembering the sympathy she'd seen in Kate's eyes when she'd talked about her father's death. She hadn't seen pity—not the kind that meant she felt sorry for her—but a warm, comforting kind of sympathy that made her feel like Kate wanted to take her pain away.

Alexi had intended to be in front of the coffee shop when Kate arrived, but she'd lost track of time. She knew the bar was a big part of her life, but she'd felt even more unfocused without it. So seeking a touchstone, she had gravitated to the garage and her father's car. The Chevelle was more than just her father's favorite car; it represented many of Alexi's fondest memories of him.

After her parents' divorce, Alexi spent two weekends a month with her father. And on those Fridays Alexi rushed home from school anticipating their time together. When after one weekend

Alexi told her mother that her father bought a new car—a new *old* car—her mother laughed and said he must be having a mid-life crisis. But Alexi didn't think it was a crisis at all. Her father had changed since the divorce, that much was certain, but for the better. He was lighter somehow, and though Alexi couldn't explain it, she could feel it. He seemed happier, and when he talked about fixing up the car there was a spark in his eyes that Alexi didn't remember seeing before.

So Alexi ignored her mother's bitterness and insisted on spending every weekend with her father. Sometimes they spent both days puttering under the hood of the car. Alexi didn't think her father knew much about fixing up cars, but she enjoyed simply spending time with him. So much so, that she didn't care that her mother complained when she came home with grease under her fingernails. She patiently endured her mother's diatribe against the death of femininity and her insistence that Alexi would never find a suitable husband by hanging around in dirty garages. Alexi's argument that knowing how to fix her own car would make her more independent didn't sway her mother's opinion of how she spent her time. Her mother was of a different generation and, to her, success meant finding a good man to take care of her. Alexi suspected her mother viewed her own divorce as her biggest failure and was afraid Alexi's life might follow a similar path.

The rattle of chain link followed the whoosh of Kate's bat through the air as the ball hit the enclosure behind her.

"Shit," Kate hissed as the next ball sailed over her swinging bat. She backed off and took a deep breath while another one passed. With renewed determination, she stepped back up to the plate.

This time she connected solidly—a line drive that shot into the net thirty yards away and fell harmlessly to the ground. Four more followed until the pitching machine ran out and she put another token in the slot.

She missed the adrenaline rush of firefighting as much as, if not more than, any other aspect of it. She also hadn't realized how much her relationship with the other firefighters would change. On the surface, they tried to treat her the same, but that was the problem; she could tell they had to make an effort. As an investigator she was still one of them, but not entirely, because she no longer entered burning buildings with them or stood behind them on the hose. She had become a peripheral part of their lives, and she had even noticed her own father and brother mentally remind themselves who she used to be when they interacted with her.

Despite her father's assertion that he understood her situation, he didn't have the same light of pride in his eyes when he looked at her. But his expression was still preferable to the pity she saw in her brother's eyes. Pity and a bit of fear. Because she was a constant example of what could still happen to him, and she was all too aware that he couldn't help but think about how it would feel to face the rest of his career unable to do what he felt he was born to do. He remained outwardly supportive, but at times Kate got the impression that he resented her for being that reminder.

In addition to the social and psychological effects, Kate was also feeling the physical fallout from her career derailment. Though most wouldn't guess it from her meticulously feminine appearance, Kate loved the manual labor of her job. She was never happier than when she was on the nozzle of a charged hose. Her duties had challenged her physically on a regular basis and now her body, confined to a desk chair, craved the exertion. So she spent her evenings at the gym or the batting cages trying to quell that need.

Today, she battled more than her usual restlessness. Her mind wouldn't stop replaying her conversations with both Alexi and Jason. Alexi Clark was difficult to read. Kate sensed Alexi's secrets ran deep and were well protected. She was an obvious suspect, but Kate's gut told her that the pain and loss in Alexi's eyes was real. That bar was so connected to Alexi's identity that she seemed very unlikely to have had anything to do with the fire. Still, Kate was certain Alexi held the key to breaking this case. Somebody had burned that bar down on purpose, not on a whim. Vandals wouldn't have taken the time to go inside and plant the chunk of concrete.

As dusk crept in and brilliant floodlights came on overhead, the rhythmic crack of her bat drove her thoughts away and she settled into a fluid motion. She continued to swing until her arms were heavy and her torso ached. When her final token ran out she pushed open the gate. At the car, she put her gear in the trunk and sucked in a breath as a twinge shot across her back. She stretched cautiously until she was convinced the pain was temporary—a product of overexertion, not injury.

Chapter Eight

Fires involving fatalities felt different than those that destroyed only property: an air of loss hung heavily over the scene. And it touched Kate the moment she stepped out of her Tahoe. She'd heard on the radio that neighbors had reported a woman and three children were trapped inside one apartment. Firefighters had been able to get to the mother and two of the kids, and Kate had met the ambulance screaming toward the hospital with one victim, critically injured, as she pulled up.

The fire had already consumed nearly half the building and still burned before her. Each unit housed a block of four apartments and was connected to the next by a breezeway. The blaze had spread quickly, and the incident commander had determined it too risky to have crews inside. Responders from several engine and truck companies continued to saturate the building from the outside, but Kate could sense a difference in their efforts. The men and women on the hoses still fought, hoped in spite of everything that they could somehow make the save. But those who had been relieved showed the truth in the slump of their shoulders as they sat on the bumpers of their engines with helmets and soaked turnout coats discarded at their feet.

Near the complex's business office a crowd of people stood staring at the building, shades of orange and yellow flickering over their shocked expressions. Kate had never gotten used to the absurd uniform of the displaced, aroused sleepers wearing whatever jacket they could grab over various types of pajamas before they fled their home. Those who hadn't had time to get a coat clutched blankets around their shoulders, which the paramedics had provided.

Kate quickly located Unit 2, the mobile-command vehicle, just as Jason appeared at the door and waved her over. He stepped down from the converted RV.

"We got the prints back on that gas can. We found Ms. Clark's and Ron and Danielle Volk's."

"That doesn't prove anything. They all had access to the garage." The information dashed Kate's hopes that someone else's prints would show up.

"I know. But I thought you would want to know the report was faxed to the office."

Kate nodded.

"Come on, they're waiting for us inside." Jason climbed back into the RV.

Kate left her turnout coat and helmet just outside and followed. Inside, the assistant chief paced the length of the narrow center of the space. He paused occasionally to speak to an administrative officer, who diligently took notes at a desk positioned along one side.

Jason slid into a booth near the front and Kate sat beside him.

"What do you have on the C side?" The assistant chief stopped and turned to one of his district chiefs, who stood near a large whiteboard affixed to the wall. The rough shape of the building was surrounded by a scrawl of shorthand that a layperson would probably find impossible to decipher. But in one glance, Kate could determine the layout of the scene outside.

"Twelve and fifteen." The district chief responded quickly and succinctly, identifying the numbers of the two engine companies assigned to cover the rear of the building. He filled the role of "Operations" and was responsible for managing the personnel who were mounting the assault on the inferno. He tracked the location of the various crews and how long they'd been working. When a crew needed relief he sent replacement companies to their position. The crew then reported to rehab, where they rehydrated and rested until they were called upon for another task.

Kate leaned forward and looked out the window. A few feet away, between the RV and the closest engine, a woman stood wrapped in a coarse gray blanket. Tears streamed down her face and she sobbed between wracking coughs. The department chaplain placed a comforting hand on her shoulder, but his presence did little to slow the pace of her tears. A rustle of movement in the opening of the blanket drew Kate's eyes. Tucked beneath the woolen folds, a girl, no more than five years old, clung to the woman's legs.

"Her other daughter didn't make it out," the chief said, looking over Kate's shoulder. When a disembodied voice over his radio notified him that representatives from the Red Cross had arrived, he instructed that they be shown to the command vehicle. The Red Cross would help the displaced families find shelter for a few nights as well as provide clothing and other personal items.

The girl tilted her head back to look up at her mother, fear and confusion etched on her small features. She said something Kate couldn't hear. But when the woman pressed the child closer in a comforting gesture, her gaze remained on the building in front of her.

After leaving the pair in the capable hands of a Red Cross volunteer, the chaplain crossed the short distance to Unit 2. As Kate studied his serious expression she wondered how it must feel to constantly be that close to such overwhelming loss. Certainly she'd witnessed the same devastation many times, and over the years, a few victims had stuck with her, but going about the urgent business of her job often kept her physically distant enough to remain somewhat detached. While in the midst of fighting the fire, she often passed off emotional family members to police officers, paramedics, or the chaplain. Only later would she allow herself to feel the mixture of loss and failure that always assailed her when she was unable to save a victim.

"Early reports indicate that the fire started on the ground floor." The chief addressed Kate and Jason, as well as the public-information officer, who would later be responsible for talking with the members of the media. "Engines nine and twelve were first on scene, and Captain Webb took her crew inside and completed a successful rescue of all but one of the residents of that apartment. They were about to re-enter for the third child, who we believe was hiding in the back bedroom, when I ordered everyone out. The building was fully involved and it was just too hot to let them back in."

Kate had heard the quick exchange between the chief and Captain Webb on the radio. Webb had not been happy about having her rescue attempt cut short, but after arguing as long as she reasonably could, she'd obeyed the order.

"I heard one of the guys say they suspected this was an electrical fire," the PIO said, looking up from his notes.

The chief glanced at him, displeasure evident on his face. "That's not for public consumption. As usual, we won't issue an official statement until the investigators confirm origin."

"We'll let you know something when we can, Chief." Jason stood and moved to the door.

Outside, Kate retrieved her gear and followed him out across the parking lot to where the bulk of apparatus clustered. Swollen hose connected hydrants to engines, then stretched toward the apartment buildings.

"There's a good chance that electrical-fire idea has already reached the media," Jason said.

"I know." If the rumor had passed through the rank of firefighters to reach the PIO, odds were that a reporter on scene had also intercepted it.

"Forget you heard it. Nothing is fact until our investigation is complete."

"Just forget it? Those guys usually know how to spot this stuff." Electrical fires were common. Kate had seen the evidence of many in her time, and she wondered why Jason would discount the opinions of experienced firefighters on scene.

"Even if it's the likely source, you should figure out how to put it out of your mind. If you're looking for electrical, you might miss something important that would lead in another direction."

Kate nodded, and when Jason stopped to talk to the EMS district chief, she took the opportunity to slip on her coat and helmet.

"Chief, what do you have?" Jason asked.

The district chief was the immediate supervisor of the medics assigned to the call. He was responsible for making sure enough units were on scene to treat and transport any victims. Standard operating procedure also dictated that one extra paramedic team be on scene at all times in case a firefighter got injured.

"I've got two units still on scene. We're already transporting three residents for smoke inhalation and two with burns, one pretty serious. And one victim we weren't able to reach."

"Has the on-call medical examiner been called?"

"She's on her way."

We've also got a paramedic from eighteen going to the hospital."

"Which one?" Kate asked, the mention of her old station ringing warning bells.

"Stocks."

"Damn it. Paula," Kate muttered. "Is she okay?"

"Yeah, she took in some smoke. They were one of the first medic crews on scene and went in to help an elderly woman out of one of the rear apartments. Saved her life, but they'll catch hell when we get done here."

Paramedics weren't equipped to enter building fires. But neither the lack of protective gear or department prohibitions would have stopped Paula from trying to help that woman.

"She's being transported?"

"Yes. But I think she only agreed to go in order to escape my wrath, or delay it at least."

Kate nodded. She scanned the scene, checking to see if the medic unit had left yet. She spotted an ambulance across the parking lot, but another vehicle blocked the number on its side.

"You can go check on her if you want to," Jason said as they headed toward the building where the fire originated.

"That's okay." Kate forced her mind back to the investigation. Smoke inhalation was common among firefighters, and they usually had to report to the hospital as a precaution.

"Hey." Jason stopped her with a hand on her shoulder. "I know it's not a big deal. But if it was one of my buddies I'd want to see if they need anything. Besides, this is most likely only a lot of paperwork. After all, it was just an electrical fire."

"I thought we were supposed to forget that."

"Just go." He shoved her away gently. "Do what you gotta do. I'll take care of this."

"Thanks."

"When you get to the hospital, see if you can get any info on the residents that were transported from here. We'll need to interview them later."

"I'll probably just be sitting around with Paula anyway. I'll try to knock out a couple of the interviews."

"Great. Make sure you check on that critical child. If she doesn't make it, we'll need to document her death."

"No problem." Kate strode across the lot already planning her own lecture for Paula.

As Kate drew closer, she spotted Paula through the open rear doors of the ambulance. From the way she was perched on the edge of the stretcher it looked like she was planning to flee at any moment. A paramedic sat opposite her taking her blood pressure.

"So is it true that paramedics make the worst patients?" Kate asked as she climbed into the back of the ambulance.

"Yes," the man treating Paula answered without hesitation.

"No." Paula pulled the oxygen mask away from her face.

"You need to leave that on." The paramedic shooed Paula's hand away and replaced the mask. He leaned toward the front where his partner sat in the driver's seat. "We're ready to roll."

"I'll follow you." Kate squeezed Paula's hand, then released it.

"I'm okay," Paula said. "I'll probably be back at the station before my crew is released from the scene."

"Good. Then you'll need a ride *home*." Kate didn't intend to let Paula return to finish her shift. "I'll meet you at the hospital." Kate didn't wait for her to argue further. She jumped down from the ambulance and closed the back doors.

Kate left her Tahoe near the emergency entrance out of the way of incoming ambulances and hurried to the door just as Paula was being pushed in on the stretcher. As they passed a large semicircular desk, the paramedic briefed an approaching doctor on Paula's condition.

Kate tuned out the medical terminology in favor of assessing the competence of Paula's doctor. She was a slight woman, but the shapeless green scrubs didn't reveal anything further about her build. A no-nonsense bun held her coppery hair captive, except for the strand that had escaped to fall against her cheek. As she scanned Paula from head to toe, her smoky eyes were sharp and intelligent, and somehow Kate knew they didn't miss a thing in their quick appraisal.

"Take her to room three." Not originally from the South, Kate guessed from the staccato words that matched the doctor's demeanor as she followed the stretcher to the examination room.

Grateful that her uniform spared her from any questions about her presence, Kate stepped in behind them and immediately moved to the side, out of the way.

"I really don't need to be here," Paula said as the paramedics transferred her to the hospital gurney.

"You'll be in enough trouble when the chief gets his hands on you, Stocks," one of the medics said as they wheeled their stretcher out. "So just be quiet and let the doc examine you."

The doctor reeled off a string of tests for the nurse to order and waited while Paula's vitals were taken.

"Doctor—" Paula dropped her eyes to the identification tag clipped to the doctor's breast pocket—"Fields, we bring patients here all the time, and I don't remember seeing you before."

"I just started here this week." She rested a hand on Paula's shoulder and slipped the end of her stethoscope under the hem of Paula's shirt.

"What do you think, am I going to make it?"

"Shh. Take a deep breath."

When Paula inhaled then began coughing, she flushed. Dr. Fields pulled the stethoscope from her ears.

"Sorry," Paula murmured.

"I want to keep you on the oxygen for a bit longer, but I don't hear anything to be concerned about." Dr. Fields replaced the mask with a nasal canula and reduced the flow of oxygen. "We'll give you a breathing treatment, too. Someone will be in to get your history and start a chart. I'll be back to check on you in a bit."

"Do you think you'll need to keep me overnight?"

Dr. Fields paused in the doorway, her brow furrowed in confusion. "Overnight? Certainly not."

"I thought you might want to—observe me."

If the doctor picked up Paula's suggestive tone, she didn't give any indication. "You'll be out of here in a little while."

"Did you catch that?" Paula asked Kate after Dr. Fields had gone. She leaned precariously off the edge of the bed in an effort to see into the hallway.

"What?" Kate crossed to Paula's side. "You're going to fall off there."

Paula straightened. "Couldn't you feel the sexual tension between us?"

"What are you talking about? She barely noticed you."

"Ha. She was trying to make it seem that way."

"Convincingly, too."

Paula twisted her hands together nervously. "She's cute."

"Are you blushing?"

"No."

"Yes, you are." Kate grinned. "You're smitten."

"Oh, come on, Kate. Nobody says that anymore."

"They do if it's true."

"Shut up."

Kate smiled. If Paula really was attracted to Dr. Fields, she may have met her match, because the doctor didn't seem the least bit interested.

Kate pushed the Up button on the elevator and stepped back to wait for the car. While Paula was receiving an albuterol treatment, Kate had excused herself to check on the other victims from the fire. In the Emergency Department, she had collected contact information and brief statements from those with minor injuries. When she had inquired at the desk about the critically injured child the clerk informed her that the child had already been transferred to the Pediatric ICU. She was on her way up there now.

The nurse downstairs said that the girl had been unconscious when she was sent up, but Kate hoped to find a family member or additional witness waiting upstairs. When the doors opened, Kate entered and shifted to move behind the three other occupants. Two doctors in scrubs conferred quietly about a patient's bypass surgery. The other passenger, a teenager dressed in all black, leaned against the wall opposite Kate as if she wished she could fade into it. When the car stopped at the next floor, all three exited, leaving Kate alone to ride up the remaining two floors. Seconds later, the doors slid back. Kate bypassed the nurses' station and headed down the hallway.

She paused in front of a glassed-in pediatric intensive-care room and consulted her notes. At three years old, the girl was the youngest victim of the fire. She looked small and defenseless nestled in the sterile white linens. Wires crossed her inert body and connected to machines at her bedside that sent a continuous stream of information back to the nurses' station. Kate watched the heartbeat jump as it scrolled across the screen, tiny peaks that didn't adequately describe the miracle of the heart pumping inside that little chest. Bandages spotted with blood obscured one side of her face.

"They're keeping her sedated."

Kate turned at the quietly spoken words from behind her. The woman standing there stared past Kate and into the room beyond. Her eyes were red and welled with tears as she looked at the girl. The disheveled state of her short gray hair and the way her clothes seemed to have been haphazardly thrown on gave Kate a hint that she'd been awakened unexpectedly. She clutched a wad of tissue in one fist, and her other hand shook as she touched it to her throat. She didn't even appear to notice Kate, but there was no else to whom she could have been speaking.

"Such a sweet girl. She laughs all the time." The woman finally looked at Kate and Kate almost wished she hadn't. The agony in her eyes was razor sharp and drew blood in Kate's soul. "I'm her grandmother, Lynn Keller."

"Kate Chambers. I'm an investigator with the fire department. Were you at the apartment complex when the fire started?"

"No. I live down the street. I got there just as the fire engines arrived. My daughter called me. She couldn't stand to leave until she knew all of her girls were safe."

Kate remembered the woman huddled under the blanket outside the command van. One of her daughters clung to her legs, one was in an ambulance on the way to the hospital, and the other was still inside. Kate couldn't imagine being torn in so many directions and all of them promising only pain.

❖

"How are we doing in here?" Dr. Fields asked as she strode into the room.

"Ready to go home, Doc," Paula answered as the doctor crossed to her bedside.

Dr. Fields scanned Paula's chart. "Your blood gases look fine. I don't see any reason to keep you. But if you experience any increased shortness of breath, dizziness, or nausea you should have someone bring you back in."

"I'm single," Paula blurted. "There's no one to—I mean—I can drive myself in."

"It would be better if you could have someone stay with you for the night."

"I'll stay with her," Kate said before Paula could recover sufficiently to come up with a suggestive reply.

"Good. Stop at the front desk on your way out so they can discharge you." Dr. Fields turned and swept out of the room.

Paula's eyes followed her until she turned a corner in the hallway and was no longer visible. When Kate began laughing, Paula's gaze cut quickly to her.

"What's so funny?"

"You should see your face. You look like someone just stole your puppy."

"She really didn't notice me at all, did she?"

"She seems very—focused." Kate began to gather up Paula's discarded clothes. "Get dressed."

Still sulking, Paula slid off the bed. Kate untied the back of her gown for her, then turned around while Paula changed. After leaving her card with Lynn Keller and at the nurses' station, Kate had returned to find Paula still waiting for the doctor to return. They had waited another hour before Dr. Fields came back.

"I'm ready."

Kate picked up Paula's jacket and folded it over her arm. "With all the time you spend in hospitals, it's ironic that you had to be a patient to meet a hot doctor."

"Yeah, ironic."

"Oh, stop pouting." Kate followed Paula into the hallway. "Hey, look at it this way. Maybe she hasn't realized yet that she can't live without you, but you'll be seeing her again when you bring patients here. That will give you plenty of time to sneak up on her."

"You may be right about that. Can you drop me by the station?"

"You should go home and rest."

"My truck is there."

"I'll take you over tomorrow to get it. Besides, your chief as much as told me he would have your ass when you got back. Are you really in a hurry to get your dressing-down?"

"I guess that's reason enough to wait till tomorrow." Paula stopped at the emergency-room desk and signed the appropriate forms.

"What were you thinking, going inside, anyway?" Kate asked as they picked their way through the crowded waiting room.

"I know you big, bad firefighters think we paramedics should stand on the sidelines and let you be the heroes, but—"

"Paula, you know I don't believe that." Kate fished her keys out of her jacket pocket and disarmed her alarm. She opened the passenger door, but Paula didn't get in. Instead she turned to Kate.

"The two crews on scene were already pulling victims from the building when we saw an old woman trying to get out. I was only in there for a second."

Kate waited until Paula settled in, then closed the door and circled the car.

"A second was long enough to land you in the hospital," Kate said when she was behind the wheel.

"Oh, please, they didn't even admit me."

"That's no excuse."

"I've transported firefighters in worse shape, and they were supposedly wearing gear at the time."

"That's exactly my point. You could have been seriously injured."

"But I wasn't. So why are we arguing about it now?"

Kate sighed in frustration with Paula's stubbornness. "Just promise me you won't do it again."

"I can't promise you that." Paula covered Kate's hand on the gearshift and squeezed. "But thank you for worrying about me."

Chapter Nine

Alexi sat in her car outside Tony's Place staring at the front door. As the only other sports bar in the downtown area, Tony's was technically Alexi's closest competitor, but Alexi seriously doubted they shared any customers. She'd been sitting here for twenty minutes, and the few people who went inside didn't look like they'd ever been in her bar. Alexi's place was several blocks closer to Broadway and she had attracted more tourists. Finally deciding she couldn't sit in the parking lot all day, Alexi got out and crossed the cracked asphalt.

Anthony Wilde had run this place for over two decades, and the exterior of the building didn't appear to have had an upgrade in that time. Alexi couldn't see through the layer of grime that blanketed the two small windows, and many of the brown wooden shingles that covered the front were rotted and falling off. Several simple cosmetic changes could certainly improve its appearance, but Alexi suspected the clientele didn't come here for the décor.

Alexi pulled open the door and paused just inside while her eyes adjusted to the lighting change. The glow from several televisions and a sparse row of pendant lights scattered across the center of the room provided the only illumination in the dark interior. As the shadows cleared, Alexi could make out several figures hulking over the bar. She headed in that direction but glanced at the men only cursorily. Instead, she directed her statement to the bartender.

"Let him know Alexi Clark is here to see him, please."

The man nodded silently and picked up a phone behind the bar. He turned his back to her, then moments later waved her toward a door to her right.

Since he still hadn't spoken to her, Alexi saw no need to respond. She tapped on the door and waited until a voice from within beckoned her to enter. She stepped inside and closed the door behind her. This office had obviously received more attention than the rest of the business. The carpet was plush and the furnishings expensive. Behind the large ornate desk a sizable man filled a well-padded office chair.

"Good afternoon, Ms. Clark. Please, have a seat. What brings you to my fine establishment?" His voice was rough, as if he'd smoked far too many cigarettes. His jet black hair was slicked back, and his garish purple silk shirt overpowered his tailored gray blazer. Alexi nearly laughed when she noticed the thick gold chains inside his open collar. Anthony Wilde was a cliché of his own making. He obviously wanted to be a mobster, but he had absolutely no connections. Instead he was only a small-town bookie with little or no influence outside of this building, let alone the city.

"Well, Mr. Wilde, since you were kind enough to send two of your men to my bar, I thought I should treat you to a visit as well."

"I certainly don't dictate where my associates choose to spend their leisure time." He raised his hands in a gesture of innocence that Alexi wasn't buying. "Just as you obviously have no control over how your partner spends his."

"What do you know about my partner?"

"I think we both know what I'm talking about. So let's not insult your intelligence or mine by pretending we don't."

"I don't approve of Ron's gambling. But he's a big boy, and whatever he owes you is between you and him. It has nothing to do with my business."

"I agree."

"So you're telling me you have no idea how a fire started in my bar."

Anthony enfolded one large hand inside the other and leaned forward, resting his elbows on the desk in front of him. "Your pal Ronnie is down a lot of money and, yeah, I sent the boys over to remind him of his debt. But arson is not my style."

Alexi leaned forward as well and met his eyes. Bloodshot with heavy folds beneath them, they reminded Alexi of a basset hound's. "Is it possible someone may have acted on your behalf without your approval?"

"No."

She wasn't entirely convinced. But those two idiots he'd sent didn't seem like independent thinkers. If they did come up with an idea like arson, they probably would be quick to brag to the boss about their exploits.

"Thank you for stopping by, Ms. Clark. If I hear anything about your bar, I'll be sure to let you know. After all, we small-business owners need to stick together."

Alexi certainly didn't believe that he was sincere. But she stood, allowing him to dismiss her. She had all the information she was going to get today. She needed to regroup and figure out her next step.

❖

After Kate dropped Paula off at home with a promise to check on her in a few hours, she drove back to the office. Jason had returned from the scene and was busy cataloging the evidence he'd collected. He'd determined that the fire had started in the bedroom of a ground-floor apartment and was electrical in origin. Kate began to sort through his notes and enter them into the software they used to generate reports while he uploaded the photographs from his digital camera.

As Kate read Jason's account of the scene, the image of the mother and daughter kept returning to her. Again, Kate mulled over the fact that throughout her years as a firefighter, with only a few exceptions, she'd conditioned herself to look past the displaced residents. From the time she jumped down from the engine, every second counted, and she couldn't afford to get caught up in feeling sorry for the families clustered outside.

But this morning, without an urgent purpose and the adrenaline singing through her blood, Kate had been more aware of the details she usually missed. She'd noticed how the little girl clinging to her mother's legs looked scared as she watched the firefighters in heavy gear hurrying around them. Did the blanket feel scratchy against the little girl's face as she peeked out from under it? The mother had cradled a hand on the back of her daughter's head as the chaplain told her they had been unable to save her other child. The woman's tears left tracks down her cheeks, and when the chaplain placed a comforting hand on her shoulder she leaned into his touch as if drawing strength. Kate had barely paid attention to the things she normally did, such as hose diameters, building construction, and attack-team placement. She also hadn't searched the crowd of apparatus for familiar faces.

Her thoughts returned to the grandmother staring into that hospital room as if she would willingly give her own life to ensure that the child survived. These were the people Kate was accustomed to helping. But what could she do now that the rescuing was done and the fire was out?

"Sit here behind a desk," she mumbled. "That's what I can do."

"What?" Jason asked from his desk a foot away.

"Nothing."

When Kate finished entering Jason's notes, she printed the various reports, then leaned back in her chair and sighed. Jason grabbed the pages as the printer spit them out.

"We'll still have to do a little legwork to confirm everything, but it looks like the fire was accidental."

"That's a whole lot of paperwork for one case," Kate said.

"It always is when there's a fire death." Jason flipped through the pages. "We create our own file and send copies to headquarters and the medical examiner's office."

"I've never seen it from this side."

"It still gets to you. But I don't think this is as difficult as being the guys out there on the trucks."

"Really? Because being in this office is harder for me. I feel like I'm getting overloaded with the emotional aspects that I used to be able to shut out. And I don't have that physical outlet any longer."

"This job is definitely an adjustment. Don't put too much pressure on yourself to make that transition quickly. Stepping away from your emotions isn't as easy when you've been in the victims' homes and seen the pieces of their lives destroyed."

Kate nodded. "Sometimes I felt like I could have done something more to get them out. But at least when I was on the engine, at the end of the day I was so exhausted I knew I'd done all I could, and that helped take the sting out of the losses. How did you deal with the ones you couldn't save when you were on a truck?"

"I went home and hugged my kids." Jason was a father of four, three boys and a girl. He joked that his wife let him stop after their daughter because he'd finally gotten it right. "What do you do?"

Kate shrugged. "I used to go a round or two on the heavy bag in the truck bay, or have a drink at the Blue Line with the guys. Sometimes I'd talk to my dad or my brother."

"You can still do all of that."

Kate shrugged. "I'm not sure they would understand my complaints about this job as well as they did before."

"I'll have a drink with you anytime you need one."

"Thanks, I appreciate that."

"You're lucky to have family in the department."

"I guess, but they like to think they're tough guys. They don't really like to talk about feelings and stuff. But it doesn't seem like anyone else can understand the things we've seen."

"They can't." Jason picked up the photo of his family from his desk and smiled faintly as he looked at them. The love he had for them warmed his eyes. "My wife tries, she really does. But I don't need her to get it."

"Why not?"

"Because back then that's what my crewmates were for. Those guys who went in with me knew what I felt, and that was enough. My family is my escape, and knowing I could help keep the ugliness in the world away from them for a while longer is what allowed me to go on the next call."

"I visited your friend Anthony Wilde today." Alexi sat on the sofa in Ron and Danielle's condo and carefully watched Ron's reaction. His expression tightened but Alexi saw no other outward signs of stress. He stood across the room leaning an elbow on the fireplace mantle in what felt like forced casualness.

"I told you I would take care of it."

"Aren't you concerned he may have had something do with the fire?"

"Not in the least."

"Does Danielle know what's been going on?"

"No."

"You should tell her."

"Tell me what?" Danielle asked from behind Alexi. Panic flashed across Ron's face before he quickly masked it.

He crossed to Danielle's side. "Nothing to worry about, darling. Alexi is just a little stressed lately."

"Of course, I'm stressed." Alexi stood quickly. "My life is falling apart and I can't do anything about it."

"What did you want him to tell me?" Danielle asked.

Alexi looked at Ron, waiting for him to speak up, but he didn't. He put his arm around Danielle and eased her closer, as if to emphasize whose side Danielle was likely to take. Alexi decided the time for secrecy had passed. If they ever hoped to move forward, they needed to have more honest communication between them.

"Ron has been taking money from the bar to pay off gambling debts."

"Are you out of your mind?" Ron strode forward and got in Alexi's face, but she refused to flinch.

"I had your back until—"

"Where do you get off—"

"You crossed a line when you started stealing from me—"

"I already knew." Danielle's quiet statement stopped them both in mid-argument.

"What did you—how did…"

If Alexi hadn't been in total shock herself, Ron's stuttering response might have been comical.

"I'm not an idiot, Ron. I knew you were gambling long before you started taking money from the business accounts. But, silly me, I thought if I pretended I didn't see it, it would go away. I didn't want to believe you could let it go this far, that you would jeopardize our future. And look at us now." Danielle swiped angrily at her tears.

Alexi took a step toward her, intending to offer comfort, but reconsidered when Danielle glared at her.

"And you. You're supposed to be *my* friend. How could you keep this from me?"

"I was only trying to protect you." Alexi moved forward again and touched Danielle's shoulder.

"I had a right to know what was going on. I shouldn't have had to find out on my own." Danielle shrugged off Alexi's hand.

"He promised me it wouldn't happen again."

"Obviously, it did."

Alexi glanced at Ron, who still stood across the room fidgeting. "Yes."

"And you think these people had something to do with the fire?" Danielle asked.

"I don't know. I went to see his bookie today and—"

"Alexi! That was a dangerous thing to do."

"Oh, please. I'm not afraid of some wannabe tough guy."

"Maybe you should be, if you really think he's capable of arson."

Alexi remembered how intimidating Anthony Wilde had tried to look, but he had obviously been bluffing. She hadn't crossed him off her list of suspects yet, but her gut told her that he didn't have it in him.

"Okay, listen up. Both of you." Danielle gave each of them a stern look. "No more arguing about the past. I don't intend to let this destroy us. And Alexi, you stay out of this investigation. I don't want you getting hurt. Do you understand me?"

Alexi glanced at Ron but he was staring at the floor. Alexi wasn't sure she could simply forgive Ron and move on. She'd tried that once and he'd just betrayed her again. In fact, Ron's idea to go their separate ways after they got the insurance money was beginning to sound good.

"Well?" Danielle demanded.

"I need to know what happened." Alexi couldn't promise not to continue asking questions.

"Let that investigator do her job."

Kate Chambers's face popped into Alexi's head. She'd seen unexpected strength behind Kate's serene bottle green eyes and smooth, creamy complexion. For a moment she allowed herself to wonder how it would feel to trust Kate. "I'll try." She finally relented because she knew Danielle wouldn't give up.

CHAPTER TEN

Kate shuffled forward as the customer at the front of the line went to the counter. After finishing the reports on yesterday's apartment fire, she and Jason had decided to break for lunch. She lost the coin toss and now waited for her turn at the deli several blocks from the office. She held a list of lunch orders for Jason and the other investigators wrapped around an assortment of bills.

"Next."

Kate inched closer. There was just one person in front of her when her cell phone rang. Recognizing Jason's number, she flipped it open. "Yeah?"

"Where's your pager?"

Kate clapped a hand against her hip where her pager should be and encountered only the smooth leather of her belt. "I—um—"

"It's sitting on your desk. Or, more accurately, just about vibrated itself off your desk." Before she could offer an excuse, he continued. "Dispatch put out a structure fire."

"It's not our call. Branagh and Walsh get the next one."

"I still thought you might want to know."

"Okay, go ahead." Kate pulled out a pen and wrote down the address he gave.

"Why does that sound…" When the numbers clicked in her

head, Kate stepped back quickly and nearly bumped into the man waiting in line behind her. Ignoring his look of annoyance, she rushed toward the door. "I'll meet you there."

She saw the smoke billowing up between the buildings as soon as she stepped outside. A flash of panic gave way to the calm she was always able to summon even in the most stressful situations. The need to simply do her job swelled within her, and it didn't matter that the nature of that job had changed.

Seconds later, as she pulled up in front of the still-charred shell of In Left Field, she was determinedly all business. Three engines and a truck angled in front of the building, and lines of hose snaked into the narrow entrance of the alley. Kate followed them over the cracked asphalt toward the back of the building. As she caught sight of the carriage house, Kate's heart dropped. The doors stood open, one hanging precariously on its hinges, and through the cloud of smoke and ash drifting from inside, Kate could make out the burnt shape of the Chevelle. *Oh, Alexi.*

From the end of the alley she heard raised voices and turned to investigate. Alexi argued with one of the firefighters, who obviously didn't want to let her any closer to the scene.

"Son of a bitch," Kate muttered under her breath. Taking a deep breath she walked toward the street. When Alexi saw Kate, a myriad of emotions crossed her face and Kate tried to decipher them. Confusion. Pain. And grief.

"It's okay," Kate said as she dropped a hand on the firefighter's shoulder. "Let her in."

He stepped aside and Alexi rushed forward. "What happened?" she demanded of Kate.

"I don't know. I just got here myself." Kate placed herself in front of Alexi, blocking her view of the garage, and fisted her hands at her sides to keep from reaching for Alexi's elbow. "Maybe you shouldn't go down there right now."

"No. I need to see it."

"It'll only hurt." More than anything, Kate wanted to spare Alexi the inevitable anguish.

"It won't hurt any less later." Alexi visibly drew herself up, and without waiting for Kate's approval she covered the remaining distance in the alley.

Kate followed closely and heard a soft sob when Alexi got close enough to see inside the garage. Alexi pressed a hand over her mouth and her eyes welled up.

"Alexi, I'm so sorry."

As firefighters continued to work around them, now rolling hose and packing up tools, Alexi stared at the remains of her father's car. The once-gleaming red hood was now swirled with black and varied shades of gray. Kate couldn't see the interior through the discolored and cracked glass of the windshield.

Alexi stumbled forward several steps and reached toward the front of the car.

"You can't touch anything until we've photographed it." Kate caught Alexi around the waist and held her back. She gestured toward another investigator, who moved around the interior of the garage snapping photos.

Alexi drew her hand back. "It's my car, my prints are already on it."

"We need to preserve any evidence."

"What difference does it make now?" The steel Kate had admired in Alexi only moments ago sagged into near-defeat.

Alexi trembled against Kate and, reminded that she still held her amid the crowded scene, Kate let her go. She took a step away. "Let me…" the words *help you* died in her throat.

"What? What are you going to do?" Alexi turned on her, anger burning through her tears. "You can't possibly believe I set this fire too."

Maybe that's what you want me to think. Kate immediately felt guilty at the direction of her thoughts. Of course, she didn't believe Alexi could destroy her father's car. But somehow, Alexi had still seen the idea cross her face.

"You do? You actually think I did this?"

"Alexi, wait." Kate grabbed her upper arm but released

her when Alexi flinched. "I'll make sure you have access to the garage as soon as we're done."

"Thank you," Alexi said, but the words didn't feel genuine.

"Sure." As Kate walked away she refused to examine her disappointment when the wall between them crept up several feet.

❖

Kate followed Paula through the crowd at the Blue Line, surprised to find it so busy on a Tuesday night. Kate tugged on Paula's sleeve, then moved close enough to be heard.

"Are you sure you should be out tonight?"

"Give me a break. I sat home all day yesterday and I almost went stir crazy." Paula was definitely not accustomed to being sedentary. "There's an empty table over there."

"You grab it. I'll get our drinks." Kate raised her voice to be heard over the cacophony of voices, then detoured to the bar.

"Two beers," Kate called when she caught the bartender's eye. She looked around while she waited and was surprised to see Alexi on a stool at the end of the bar. Her eyes were on the low-ball glass in front of her, and her fingers played absently around the rim.

"Aren't you on the wrong side of the bar?" Kate slid into an empty space next to Alexi.

"Not working tonight," Alexi mumbled without looking up, her words softly running together. She picked up her glass and swirled the amber liquid before draining the last swallow.

"How are you doing?"

"Just peachy."

"Listen, I'm sorry about today."

"Don't worry about it. You already thought me capable of burning down my own bar. It shouldn't surprise me that you think I torched the garage too."

"Alexi, I—I'm just doing my job," Kate said because she

didn't know what else to say. Alexi still hadn't looked at her, but misery was evident in her expression.

The bartender brought Kate's drinks, glanced guiltily at Alexi, and rushed away.

Kate leaned close to Alexi as she reached for the two bottles on the bar. "Can I buy you another?"

"You shouldn't."

Kate stiffened and drew away at the reminder that she had no reason to talk to Alexi unless it had to do with her case. "Right. Have a nice night, then." She'd intended a peace offering, but Alexi was obviously brushing her off.

She picked up her drinks and headed back to her table. She could tell by Paula's knowing smirk that she'd witnessed the exchange at the bar.

"Ouch. Shot down, huh?"

"Not exactly," Kate grumbled as she slid into her side of the booth.

"From where I'm sitting it looked like you got blown off."

"Can it." It was bad enough that Alexi didn't even seem interested in being polite, but getting flack from Paula made things worse.

"Damn, Chambers, when did you get so sensitive?"

"I'm not." Hearing the edge in her own voice, Kate forced herself to relax. "I'm sorry."

"Hey, it's okay. But you have been wound a little tight. I think you need to get laid."

"That's not the answer to everything."

"Of course not. But it sure helps."

"Yeah, well, even *if* that were true, we've already discussed why she is not a good option to fill that particular role. What about you? How do you intend to woo Dr. Fields?"

"Now that you mention it, I do have a game plan that is brilliant in its simplicity, if I do say so." Paula rested her elbows on the table and steepled her hands together.

"I can't wait to hear this."

"I'll talk all of our patients into going to her hospital. Then she'll see me several times a day."

Kate laughed. "She can't help but notice how smart and caring you are."

"Exactly." Paula smiled smugly.

"Sweetie, do you think it's ethical to convince patients to go to a certain hospital for your own personal gain?"

"Why not? It's a level-three trauma center. Where can they get better care?"

"You can't be serious."

"Okay, maybe not entirely. I can't influence where patients go. But we already take enough of them over there that I'm bound to see her. And when I do—"

"You'll turn on that amazing charm of yours. You're right, it's a great plan."

"Yeah. We'll see." Paula nudged Kate's arm. "Hey, it sounds like your friend is having some trouble over there."

Kate had been trying not to let her eyes wander back to the bar all night. But hearing Alexi's raised voice pulled them there.

"I said give me another drink." Alexi slid off the barstool and faced a big man Kate recognized as the bar owner.

"I think you've had enough, kiddo." His voice was calm but tension was evident in his rigid posture and the temper he obviously struggled to keep in check.

"I'll let you know when I'm through." Alexi stared at the older man, seemingly undaunted by his size or rapidly reddening face.

Kate watched, confused as he pinned the bartender with an angry glare. "What did I tell you?"

The bartender had the good sense to squirm and he stammered slightly when he said, "She's a grown woman, I thought—"

"I don't pay you to think." He turned back to Alexi. "And you—"

"Now wait just a damn minute." Alexi was not backing

down, so Kate jumped up and rushed over, worried Alexi might say something that would push him into firing her.

"Alexi, there you are. Sorry I'm late." She put an arm around Alexi's shoulders.

"What?" Alexi stared at Kate and tried to push her away.

"Well, I'm here now. So we can head out." Kate held her tight. She glanced at the owner. "Unless you need another minute."

"Get her out of here," he said, then walked away, shaking his head.

Kate steered Alexi toward the door. "Come on. I'll give you a ride."

"I can get myself home."

"Let's just get you out of here while you still have a job."

"Least of my worries right now." Then, as if to herself, Alexi mumbled, "Fucked up a year of sobriety."

"Where's your car?" Kate asked as they stepped onto the street. She could drive Alexi home, then take a cab back down here for her own car.

"Walked. Just live over there." Alexi flung an arm out, and if Kate hadn't reacted quickly enough she would have been hit in the face.

"Okay. We'll take mine." She led Alexi to her Altima.

When Alexi tried to jerk out of Kate's grasp, Kate wrapped one arm around her waist and opened the passenger door. Once Alexi was seated she shut the door and hurried around to the other side before Alexi tried to escape. Kate started the engine, then steered into the street, while Alexi slumped silently in the seat staring out the window as if the fight had suddenly gone out of her.

"Do you want to talk about it?" Kate asked quietly. *A year of sobriety?* There was more to this story and Kate needed to hear it. Several questions clustered in her mind, but she couldn't sort out which were business-related and which were personal. She'd been having that problem a lot lately where Alexi was concerned.

When Kate didn't get an answer from the other side of the car, she glanced over to find Alexi resting against the door, asleep or passed out. Making a quick decision she changed direction and headed toward her own apartment.

Minutes later, she pulled into a spot near the front of her building and gently touched Alexi's shoulder. But when Alexi only moaned softly, Kate got out and circled the car, then opened the passenger door slowly.

"Alexi." She still didn't get a response as she bent to slip a shoulder under Alexi's arm. She managed to ease Alexi from the car and get the door closed, then wrapped an arm around her torso, her hand coming to rest just under her breasts. Alexi's lean body felt even thinner than Kate had originally thought, and Kate could distinguish the distinct ridges of her ribs.

"Kate?" The confusion and vulnerability in Alexi's voice touched Kate.

"I've got you." She led Alexi up the stairs to her door, fumbling to get her keys out of her pocket. "Just a few more steps."

Alexi draped her arm across Kate's chest and turned her face into Kate's neck, making it even more difficult for Kate to maneuver as she shoved open the door.

"My head hurts," Alexi moaned as Kate awkwardly shuffled them both inside. The words vibrated against Kate's skin and warmth spread in her belly. She tightened her arm around Alexi. Protective. *I'm feeling protective toward her, that's all.*

She considered the inappropriateness of her actions for only a moment before she led Alexi into her bedroom. She'd get her settled, give her some aspirin and water, then retire to the couch.

Alexi stumbled into the center of the room, looked at the bed, and turned to Kate. "Are we going to bed?"

"You are." Kate pushed back the covers and Alexi climbed in with little urging.

Alexi caught Kate's wrist. "What about you?" She slid her hand down, entwining her fingers in Kate's.

She tugged lightly, but the motion was enough to pull Kate off balance. Kate caught herself and sat on the edge of the bed, her weight on the mattress drawing Alexi closer to her.

"I'm not very tired right now."

"Me either." Alexi got to her knees on the bed and wrapped her arms around Kate's neck. She played her fingers lightly against Kate's skin.

"You lay down." Though Kate didn't want to, she gently removed Alexi's arms. "I'm going to sleep on the couch."

"Why? Your bed is big enough for both of us." Alexi touched Kate's face. "You could just get comfortable in here." Alexi teased open the top button of Kate's shirt.

Kate caught her hands before they could make much progress and held them. "You should get some rest." Kate urged Alexi to lie down again and she complied without argument. Kate pulled the covers over Alexi's shoulders and, unable to help herself, lightly stroked Alexi's temple.

"Sleep." Alexi closed her eyes with a sigh.

Kate wondered if she should help Alexi undress, the desire to make her comfortable warring with respect for Alexi's privacy. She couldn't deny her own attraction, and so she was even more reluctant. There were lines here she couldn't cross.

"Oh, this was not a good idea," Alexi said, pressing a hand to her head.

"You couldn't be more right," Kate murmured, though she knew they weren't talking about the same thing.

"I was so close." Alexi's whisper sounded rough. Kate could imagine the pain of air passing over a tender throat burned by alcohol.

"To what?" Kate continued to circle her fingers above Alexi's brow, and Alexi pressed into her touch.

"Control."

"Is that important?"

Alexi rolled onto her side, curving her body around Kate's. "It's crucial."

"You'll probably have a headache in the morning." If she truly hadn't had a drink in a year, she would definitely have a lot more than that. But now was not the time to question Alexi further about her sobriety. "I'll get you some aspirin."

When Kate stood, Alexi curled further into a ball and tucked her fisted hands beneath her chin.

Chapter Eleven

Alexi awoke disoriented. She wasn't in her own bed, that was certain, but beyond that she didn't have a clue. The room around her offered little hint as to her whereabouts. The cappuccino headboard, bureau, and nightstands were contemporary in design, and the pristine white bedding smelled like fresh flowers. She sat up and pain speared through her head and settled behind her eyeballs. Her mouth was dry and the familiar sour taste was sickening. It had been so long since she'd awakened like this. And she hadn't missed it.

Shoving aside the sheet, she swung her legs over the side of the bed. Her bare legs. *Where are my pants?* She was wearing only a navy blue T-shirt and her panties. The shirt offered a clue in the form of a colorful logo and the words Nashville Fire Department in white letters.

"Shit," she mumbled, covering her face with her hands.

The events of the previous night trickled back and Alexi's face warmed with shame. After she'd lost her bar, she tried to take comfort in the knowledge that at least she still had the garage and her father's car. Trying to figure out what happened had consumed her so thoroughly that she had found it marginally easier to deal with everything else falling down around her. But now, her worst-case scenario had become reality, and as she'd stared at the smoldering garage, she had felt the rope of her sanity slipping through her hands. When she was finally allowed inside and saw the damage up close, her grip became even more tenuous.

Several hours later she practically barricaded herself inside her apartment, every nerve ending screaming in agony and clamoring for the numbness she knew she could find in the bottom of a bottle. She was terrified that if she left the safety of her alcohol-free apartment, she wouldn't be able to resist the urge to deaden that pain. But as she paced the hardwood floor, the walls began to press in on her and her chest constricted until she could barely breathe.

Eventually she fled, and, though she couldn't admit it at the time, that was the moment she surrendered to old demons. First, she went back to her bar. The firefighters were gone and, though the roof of the garage was still mostly intact, the alley looked emptier. The doors wouldn't close and she hadn't bothered to even try to secure them earlier, since there was no longer anything inside worth stealing.

She touched the hood of the car, almost expecting to caress the smooth, highly buffed finish. The metal felt rough, and when she pulled her hand away her fingers were smeared with soot. The pain in her chest grew and spread into her stomach and, sobbing, she dropped to her knees. She wasn't sure how long she stayed there before she pulled herself back to her feet and covered the few blocks to the Blue Line. And that's where Kate had found her two hours and far too many drinks later.

She remembered arguing with Kate in the bar, but after that things got fuzzy. This wasn't the first time she'd awakened in a strange bed with no idea how she got there. But realizing Kate was the one in the next room made her even more ashamed than those mornings when she faced a nameless stranger. She wondered if, by some miracle, she could manage to sneak out without confronting Kate, then pretend this never happened.

Of course, since she couldn't escape in her panties and Kate's

T-shirt, her first priority was to locate her clothes. She spotted her jeans neatly folded on a chair and hurriedly pulled them on. Then seeing her cell phone on the nightstand she dove for it.

"Coffee?" She heard the question from behind her just as her fingers closed around it.

She turned and forced herself to meet Kate's eyes. Dressed in dark blue jeans and a crisp, pale pink button-down shirt, Kate looked maddeningly put together, and Alexi hated how frumpy she suddenly felt. She couldn't even imagine what she might have said or done the night before. Averting her eyes, she flipped open her phone but the screen remained black. "Did—um—did you take off my clothes?"

"Actually, you did. I went to the kitchen for some aspirin, and when I came back you had stripped down to your panties."

"So we didn't—"

"No." Kate smiled and a light blush colored her cheeks. "But I had a heck of a time wrestling you into that T-shirt."

Embarrassed, Alexi looked away. The old Alexi had been known to shed her clothes pretty quickly after a night of partying. At least she'd left her panties on this time. Since she figured Kate wasn't exaggerating, she decided to change course rather than argue the point. "My cell is dead. If you'll let me use your phone I'll call a cab."

Kate stepped closer, and Alexi stared at her hands as Kate plucked away the phone and replaced it with a thick ceramic mug. "I'll drive you home."

"That's not necessary."

"I insist."

"Really, I think I should—"

"Look, I'll admit this is an unorthodox situation, considering our—um—circumstances. But it's really not a problem. I'll drive you home."

When Alexi met Kate's eyes, she didn't see the expected smug satisfaction, nor did she find even a hint of judgment. Instead, she encountered only a steady calm and a part of her wanted to surrender to Kate's confidence, even while the rest of her railed against needing anything from Kate.

"Okay." Uncertain what to do next, Alexi stood in the middle of Kate's bedroom and rubbed her hands nervously around the outside of the warm mug.

"So how does it work exactly?" Kate asked casually as she sank down on the edge of the bed. "A bartending alcoholic. It seems like that would be difficult."

Past mistakes still lingering in her mind, Alexi reacted quickly and without thought. "That's none of your business."

A bartending alcoholic. Despite knowing that both of those words did in fact define her, Alexi hated to hear her life reduced to a catchphrase. She strode out of the room and into a short hallway that led her to the living room. A folded blanket and pillow on the couch hinted that Kate had slept there.

"Relax. We're off the record." Kate entered the room behind her and moved the stack of linens to a nearby chair, then settled on the couch. Her nonchalance only further stoked Alexi's anger. "Sit." Alexi remained standing with her arms folded stiffly across her chest. "Please," Kate added softly. She didn't seem to notice that Alexi flinched when she took her hand and drew her to the sofa.

Their knees touched as they angled toward each other. Kate released her hand abruptly as if she had just realized she still held it. It occurred to Alexi that sitting in Kate's living room after having slept in her bed was not exactly appropriate behavior, considering Kate was investigating her for arson, but she could hardly undo last night now. She sipped her coffee slowly, procrastinating for a moment longer.

"Yes. It can be hard sometimes."

"Then why do it?"

"What was my alternative? Just walk away from all of my plans. Abandon my partner and the place we've built because I chose to stop drinking." She'd been committed to the bar, to Ron, apparently more than he had ever been.

"I'm sure he would understand."

Alexi shook her head, then winced as the slow throb intensified. "Damn, I don't miss hangovers," she said to herself.

"Alexi," Kate said softly. She lifted her hand as if to touch Alexi's shoulder, then let it drop back on her own thigh. Instead, she stood and walked into the kitchen.

"I'm not just talking about a business here, Ms. Chambers." Alexi raised her voice slightly in order to be heard.

"Why can't you call me Kate?" Kate came back into the living room and held out an aspirin bottle and a glass of water.

Alexi took the bottle and shook out several pills. She ignored Kate's question, refusing to admit that she needed the added distance of the more formal address. "The bar is my life. I worked for years to get my own place and finally be my own boss. And I'll fight as hard as I have to for it."

"No matter what it costs you?"

"Yes." Alexi didn't hesitate. Thinking about the series of AA meetings she would attend in atonement, she said, "Don't worry. I'll pay for what I did last night."

"Give yourself a break. You've had a rough week. It's understandable that you might have a moment of weakness."

"Life is full of rough days, Ms. Chambers. None of them is a valid excuse to drink."

"That's a pretty sanctimonious statement from someone who tied one on last night."

Alexi surged to her feet. For a moment she'd thought maybe she was wrong about Kate, that maybe Kate could understand why the bar meant so much to her. "I think we're done here. Thank you for—your hospitality, but I need to get home now."

Kate caught Alexi at the door and grasped her elbow. "Wait."

Alexi turned back toward Kate, and the confines of the small foyer pushed them closer together than was comfortable.

"I'm sorry," Kate said softly. Her fingers were warm on

Alexi's arm and the compassion in her eyes pulled Alexi in. "I admit, I don't know what it's like to be in your shoes—"

"No," Alexi snapped, then forced a more neutral tone. "You don't."

Though Alexi's expression remained stoic, Kate witnessed the struggle in her expressive eyes. There she found the only hint of vulnerability in Alexi's rock-hard shell. Kate slid her hand down to grasp Alexi's and was surprised when Alexi didn't pull away. "But I can't understand unless you talk to me."

"Are you hoping I'll say something to incriminate myself?"

"Damn it, Alexi. This—right now—isn't about that." This was about Kate's overwhelming urge to embrace Alexi and absorb her pain. Despite just how much she shouldn't want to, she couldn't forget Alexi's arms around her the night before and yearned for them again. She'd gone to sleep on the couch gripped with the image of Alexi's face just before she drifted off, when the weight of her problems didn't touch her serene features. And her first thought this morning had been of Alexi. Then she felt guilty because she derived so much pleasure from thinking about Alexi lying in her bed.

"Isn't it? Can you separate the past from right now, when you're still not sure I'm innocent?"

Just then Kate wanted more than anything to believe that Alexi didn't have anything to do with the fire. She'd tucked this woman into bed last night and was certain she hadn't imagined the helpless anguish in Alexi's eyes. How could she still harbor even an inkling of suspicion? Because it was her job to be suspicious, and maybe she was fooling herself if she thought she could read Alexi.

"I…" She couldn't explain her conflicting thoughts.

"I get it," Alexi said, squeezing Kate's hand. "On paper, I probably look like a good suspect."

Alexi slipped her hand away before Kate could completely absorb the warmth of her fingers. Kate let the connection go because she'd had no right to make it in the first place. She took a half step backward, putting what little space between them that she could.

"So what now?" she asked.

"Now, you can call me a cab."

"I told you I would take you home."

"Now, you can call me a cab," Alexi repeated.

"Will you be okay? I mean, about what happened last night."

Alexi nodded. "I need to call my sponsor. And later I'll go to a meeting."

Kate knew that restoring the professional distance between them was probably the smartest course for both of them. But she couldn't forget how defenseless Alexi looked last night curled up in her passenger seat, or the way the tension strung between them softened briefly in the intimacy of her bedroom, or the way Alexi's hand felt in hers just now.

Alexi steered the Cadillac into the parking lot of the church she'd attended as a child. The stone steps had loomed large when she was young. She would stand on the sidewalk in front, tilt her head back, and stare up at the twin spires until she felt dizzy.

As a rebellious teen, she'd been forced through those doors by her mother, despite her father's insistence that Alexi should be allowed to choose whether she wanted to attend. Her mother was active in the choir and taught vacation bible school. The church had been a means of salvation for Alexi's mother through the divorce, and Alexi understood now that her mother had been trying to instill in her the same kind of faith. For Alexi, the concepts had always been rather vague. She believed in God, but when she heard her mother go on about the Holy Spirit, she never truly felt like she got it, like she knew Him.

Later, in her early twenties, she became apprehensive every time she entered the building. She'd heard the minister talking about homosexuals, and she worried that he could tell by looking at her that she was a sinner. The gap between Alexi and her higher power widened. But Alexi didn't abandon the final thread of her faith until her father died.

A year ago, when Alexi had been completely lost, she'd ended up at her first Alcoholics Anonymous meeting in the basement of this very church. Ironically, she found salvation here after all. Now Alexi stood on the sidewalk once more, hoping she could regain what she'd forsaken last night. She leaned back and squinted against the blinding midday sun. Somehow the gothic architecture didn't hold the wonder that it once did, but not much about the world did anymore.

Standing there ruminating on the past only delayed the inevitable, so she forced herself toward the church basement. She descended the stairs and the shame from this morning crept back into her heart. Several dozen people milled about the room, while others settled in the rows of chairs facing the front of the room. Alexi could pick out the new faces, by their apprehensive expressions and the way their eyes darted around the room as if trying to assess whether they really belonged here.

Alexi scanned the crowd until she saw her sponsor among a group clustered near the coffee urn in the back of the room, and immediately some of her stress melted away. Many months ago, Alexi had sat silently through her first three meetings and almost decided she didn't see much point in coming back for another when Jacob introduced himself. He'd asked how she was doing, if she had any questions about what she'd been hearing, and offered a nonjudgmental shoulder. Because of him, Alexi had returned, though she sat through another two meetings before she was able to convince herself to stand up and speak.

Over the course of several months, Alexi learned Jacob's story. He wasn't much older than she was, but he carried many more years in the weariness of his eyes. Like Alexi he'd started drinking in high school, but it had become a problem for him in college after an injury ended his basketball career. And since he no longer had to worry about random drug screens, he began doing meth as well. He stole from friends and family to pay for his habits until they all abandoned him. He soon ended up jobless and was evicted from his apartment. A chance encounter at a homeless shelter with the man who would one day become his sponsor finally brought him to his first meeting.

"Alexi, I'm glad you came. You really sounded upset on the phone," Jacob said as he appeared at her side. She'd called him as soon as she left Kate's and given him the short version of what had been happening to her.

"It's been rough lately. Particularly yesterday."

"You needed a meeting."

"Probably for longer than I'd like to admit. But I also needed to talk to you."

"What do you need to hear?" He smoothed a hand down the outside of her arm and grasped her hand.

She forced a smile. "That everything will be okay."

"It can be." He stopped short of making the promise she asked for.

"Can't you just say it *will* be?"

"That's up to you."

Alexi sighed.

"Alexi, you've been on this road before. The good news is, it doesn't have to be as rocky now."

"Let's hope not." Alexi remembered the night sweats, sleeplessness, and the days when she could barely function, and those were just the physical symptoms of withdrawal. She'd also been forced to face her guilt, delayed grief for her father, and self-esteem issues, all of which she still struggled with at times.

"They're about to start. Let's sit down." Jacob touched Alexi's elbow and led her to a row of folding chairs nearby.

Alexi settled beside him, shifting in the uncomfortable metal chair. The meeting facilitator introduced himself briefly, then opened the floor for anyone who wanted to speak. As Alexi listened to stories from both regular attendees and newcomers, some of her tension eased. The familiar security she felt when she went to a meeting replaced her worry over last night's relapse. She needed to absorb some of that calming energy, because before the meeting was over she'd have to make herself stand up and admit to her mistake.

Matching statues stood sentry at the entrance to the Evergreen Cemetery—armored men astride stone horses seemingly oblivious to the biting wind as it swept across their granite faces. Alexi passed between them and followed the left fork in the paved road that wound among rows of headstones of all shapes and sizes. She navigated through the cemetery easily despite the fact that she hadn't been here in years. Just after her father's death, she had visited every year on his birthday and the anniversary of his death. But in recent years, shame had kept her away from his grave far longer than she wanted to admit.

As she turned the final corner the pavement gave way to a dirt driveway. On the day of her father's burial it had been pouring down rain and this section of the road had been a mess of mud. Alexi remembered because she'd stepped in a puddle as she walked to the canopied area near her father's graveside and the cold water had spilled into her left shoe.

Today, the sky was brilliant blue and showed no sign of precipitation. Alexi got out of the car, put on her jacket, and pulled up her collar to block the gusting wind. When she reached his stone, she knelt in front of it. She'd been skeptical when Jacob suggested that after the meeting she should visit her father's grave. She didn't see how she could find any comfort in talking to a chunk of granite. But Jacob had insisted that she not think of it that way; instead, she should imagine having a conversation with him. So when she spoke, she closed her eyes and tried to picture his face. Instead of the hollow features that haunted his final days, she conjured an image of him before he got sick. His skin was smooth and youthful, and he smiled often and naturally, not in the forced way he did at the end when Alexi knew the pull of his lips was for her benefit.

"Hi, Dad. You're probably wondering where I've been. Well, you may already know this but I went a bit astray." The thought of her father witnessing her downward spiral after his death inspired a renewed rush of shame. He wouldn't be proud of who she'd become. "I've wasted a lot of time and I've been trying to make up for it. But lately, things have been more difficult."

She took a deep breath and made the confession she'd been trying to avoid. "I lost the car, Dad. There was a—um, a fire in my garage." She stopped and swallowed several times, her throat aching. Tears squeezed out between her closed eyelids and burned trails down her cold cheeks. "I know how much you loved that car and I kept it, hoping to preserve your memory. I'm so afraid I'll forget the details—like sometime I can't remember what your laugh sounded like.

"You know, Mom hasn't even called me?" Alexi's voice broke. Her mother read the newspaper faithfully every morning, believing an educated woman should be up on current events. So Alexi was confident that her mother knew what had happened at the bar, and it hurt that she hadn't called to check on her. Her relationship with her mother had been rocky following her father's death, and Alexi's drinking hadn't helped.

In her mind, Alexi had turned her father into a saint, and the only role left for her mother was that of villain. She blamed her mother for the demise of their marriage and for Alexi's own unhappiness during her childhood. Those memories of her father that she clung to became the highlights of her life. Before long, she viewed her mother's insistence on responsibility and discipline as a barrier to those carefree periods with her father. Her time with him had been drastically shortened, and while Alexi couldn't blame her mother for his death, she did hold her responsible for the time she could have had with him.

On some level, she knew she wasn't being fair, but the dark

hurt in her screamed that it was her mother's fault—that her mother had deliberately kept her from her father out of spite and jealousy. And when Alexi was drinking, her demons hadn't let her stay quiet. She'd picked fights with her mother in order to stoke her own anger. She yelled and hurled unreasonable insults at her own mother. And the more her mother tried to help her, the more Alexi shoved her away. Once, on the anniversary of her father's death, she'd actually said that she wished her mother had been the one to get sick instead of him. That was the last time her mother spoke to her.

When Alexi stopped drinking, she eventually began trying to make amends. That step was particularly rough for her. Her mother was the last person she went to, bolstered with promises of forgiveness from Danielle and Ron. But Alexi's mother hadn't granted the same clemency.

"I know she hasn't forgiven me, yet," Alexi said to her father's headstone. She dutifully called her mother once a month, hoping with each call that she would answer the phone this time. "But how can I apologize if she won't even talk to me? How can I show her I've changed?" Alexi laid her palm against the cold stone and her fingertips brushed the sharp edges of the letters carved there. She wished she could feel the warmth of her father's touch. As a girl, she would lay her hands in his large work-roughened ones. He would swing her around, and as her feet lifted off the ground, she had complete faith that he wouldn't let her fall. "I wish I could see you again." Alexi smiled a little as she thought about how full of life her father had been. He worked hard except when she visited him. During those times Alexi was the sole focus of his time. "But this isn't where I should be having this conversation, is it? You wouldn't be hanging around here. Where would you be?"

Alexi didn't have a solid belief about the afterlife. She couldn't quite get on board with her father sitting on a cloud in heaven somewhere. And it was equally disturbing to think about his soul following her around and watching her. Shortly after her father's death she tried to talk to her mother about it, but when she rejected the Pearly Gates theory, her mother freaked out and went on and on about sacrilege and Alexi's eventual destination in Hell. Alexi was left with no clear concept of what happened after her father was lowered into the ground. And it made her sad to think that might just be all there was—the end.

Chapter Twelve

Are you almost done?"

"Alexi, you do this every time," Danielle answered from the other side of the dressing-room door. "You say you want to go shopping with me and then all you do is rush me."

"Well, you've tried on a hundred outfits."

Danielle exited the dressing room and stopped in front of the three-way mirror. She studied the slim-cut gray slacks and lavender cashmere sweater. "How does this one look?"

"How much is it?" Alexi had never been one to spend a fortune on her wardrobe. She was most comfortable in jeans and a T-shirt. And being comfortable was one of the benefits of being her own boss. For Danielle, though, clothing was all about image, and the name on the label was as important as the way she looked. Even when she was just coming in to help in the bar she dressed in slacks and a nice blouse.

"It's on sale." She turned around then looked back over her shoulder into the mirror.

"No. It doesn't make your butt look big." Alexi moved to stand beside Danielle and put an arm around Danielle's shoulders. She compared their reflections and thought about what unlikely friends they were.

"You always know just what to say." Danielle smiled.

"I wish I always knew what to do."

"Okay. You've been pouting all afternoon. Out with it." Danielle turned and propped a hand on her hip.

"I have not been pouting."

"You know you're going to tell me eventually."

"I went to a meeting this morning."

"Honey, that's not a news flash." Danielle went back into the dressing room.

"I went to a meeting because I had a few drinks last night." Alexi winced as the cubicle door squeaked back open. Danielle stood there wearing only a black lace bra and the gray slacks, unbuttoned.

"Do you want to say that again?"

"Not really."

"Are you okay?"

Alexi nodded. "I will be. But if you don't go put some clothes on I can't make any promises," she teased.

Leaving the door open Danielle grabbed her blouse from a nearby hook and put it on, then stepped out of the slacks. Alexi returned to the chair by the mirrors.

"Why didn't you call me? You shouldn't have to be alone at a time like that."

"Well—I wasn't exactly alone."

"Oh, please, tell me you didn't hook up with a stranger."

"You're probably going to wish I did," Alexi mumbled.

"What?" Danielle came out of the cubicle with several garments draped over her arm.

"Are you going to get those?"

"I think so."

Alexi followed Danielle to the sales counter and waited while she made her purchases. She could feel Danielle giving her curious looks, but this was definitely not a discussion she wanted to have in front of some random retail clerk.

As they left the store and headed back into the mall, Danielle cleared her throat impatiently.

"Okay. When the fire department finally let me in the garage, I was devastated. I knew then that I wanted a drink. But I went home first, hoping I could stop myself."

"Oh, honey." Danielle touched Alexi's shoulder, but Alexi shifted her stride a half step to her right and Danielle's hand fell away.

"I was down at the Blue Line and Kate Chambers came in. Frankie was giving me a hard time about drinking in his place and she intervened. It gets a little fuzzy after that, but—"

"Chambers? That investigator?"

"That's the one."

"What was she doing there?" Disapproval was evident in Danielle's tone.

"I don't know. A lot of firefighters hang out there. The next thing I remember, I was waking up at her place this morning."

Danielle stopped in the middle of the walkway. "Have you lost your mind?"

Alexi winced at Danielle's harsh tone. "I told you, I'd had too much to drink and—"

"I'm so tired of you using that as an excuse for your actions."

"That's not fair. You know how hard I've worked to stay sober. I know drinking is not an excuse."

"Then why do you do things like this? What do I need to bail you out of this time?"

Alexi flinched. If anyone else had said the same thing she would have walked away from them without hesitation. But from Danielle she would take her beating. In the past, she had called Danielle to pick her up when she woke up in a stranger's house, and Danielle always came without asking questions. Before she bought her place downtown, more times than she could count she had asked Ron and Danielle for a ride to work when she didn't want to risk driving while intoxicated.

And Alexi recalled with shame the time Danielle came to the

police department after Alexi was stopped for DUI. Danielle had called her cousin, a lieutenant on the force, and managed to get the charges against Alexi dropped. Alexi accepted the reminder of her debt to Danielle, but the bitterness in Danielle's voice surprised her.

Danielle took a deep breath and visibly smoothed her expression. "I'm sorry. But what were you thinking?"

"I wasn't. I don't even know how it happened. One minute I was arguing with Frankie and the next I was in her car."

"So you slept with her?"

"No." Alexi rubbed two fingers against the dull ache behind her temple. "She slept on the sofa. Nothing happened between us." Nothing had happened, yet when she thought about Kate, she felt a lingering warmth and a tingle of excitement.

"I don't think you should be interacting with her on a personal level. Alexi, the woman is trying to prove you burned down your own bar."

"I know. Jesus, I know." Alexi took Danielle's arm and led her back into the flow of shoppers. They passed several novelty shops without going in. "It's not like I planned for this to happen. But she was actually kind of nice about it." Alexi recalled the tender way Kate had taken her hand and asked if she would be okay. But she also saw the flash of suspicion Kate had failed to hide.

"Nice?"

"Yes." For a moment it had seemed that Kate was genuinely concerned about her. Kate had only gotten touchy after Alexi questioned her motives. "Under different circumstances—"

"Under different circumstances what?" Danielle grabbed her arm and stopped again.

"I just mean, if we hadn't met the way we did. If she wasn't investigating a fire at my bar, I might actually find her attractive." *Might?* a voice in her head mocked. There was really no question she would—she did—find Kate attractive.

"Are you drunk now?" Danielle asked with a chuckle.

Alexi smiled. "She's smart and determined. And even you have to admit, she's gorgeous."

Danielle shrugged. "Maybe, but there's more than a broken heart at stake if things don't work out how you want them to."

"I'm not saying I'm planning to get involved with her."

"I know. Just be careful. I still don't think you can trust her. Let's go in here. I need some new shoes."

Danielle detoured into a nearby store before Alexi could respond. She wasn't certain what she would have said anyway. Of course she shouldn't trust Kate. There was no point in thinking about how things could be different, because if she'd learned anything it was that there were things she couldn't change. Kate was who she was, and that was reason enough not to get involved with her.

"Hey, I was just in the neighborhood. No. I had a few more questions about… No. I thought you might want to have dinner and… And what, you moron? You're supposed to be keeping things professional." Kate paced the parking lot outside Alexi's building, talking to herself like a crazy person. She'd gotten all the way here then realized she had no clue what she was going to say. Maybe she should just stick with the truth. "I was worried about you." God, that was worse.

She was still debating whether she should stay or leave when the door opened and Alexi stepped out. Alexi jumped and clasped a hand to her chest.

"Geez, you scared me."

"I'm sorry." Kate backed up two steps and shoved her hands in her pockets.

"What are you doing here?"

"Maybe I shouldn't have come but I—wanted to check on you."

"I'm fine."

"That's good." They stood in awkward silence for a moment while Kate searched for something to say. "Yesterday morning, I—"

"I'm sorry. Did you need something? Because I was on my way out." Alexi wrapped her brown leather jacket more tightly around her.

"Where are you going?" When Alexi scowled, Kate realized she might have overstepped. But she hadn't stopped thinking about Alexi since the day before, wondering how she was coping. "I thought you might still be feeling—er, that you might need to talk or something." Kate had never had so much trouble expressing herself.

"You were worried I would drink again." Alexi turned away and headed toward her car. Kate fell in step behind her and hurried to keep up.

"I know you've been through a lot recently."

"God, the last thing I need is you feeling sorry for me." Alexi stopped so quickly that Kate had to grab her shoulders to keep from running into her. She still ended up pressed a little too closely against Alexi's back.

"I'm not feeling sorry for you." Kate released her.

"Yes, you are," Alexi said as she turned to face Kate. "Maybe you should come with me."

"Sure. I can do that." Kate pulled her keys out of her pocket. "Where to?"

"I'm driving." The alarm on the Cadillac disarmed with a chirp. "Get in."

Kate reached for the passenger-door handle and paused when her eyes met Alexi's over the top of the car. Alexi seemed in good spirits, but shadows still lingered in her eyes. *I wish I could do something about that.* Kate shook away the inappropriate thought and lowered herself into the car.

"Do you intend to tell me where we're going or is it a surprise?" Kate asked as she clicked on her seat belt.

"A little drive in the country."

Kate waited for further explanation but Alexi didn't offer any. So Kate settled into the supple leather seat and enjoyed the ride. On the interstate, they quickly left the city behind. The billboards became sparse and Kate began to see exits for suburban areas.

Alexi glanced over but Kate was staring out the passenger side window. She wasn't sure what had compelled her to invite Kate along today. Truthfully, she'd been caught off guard to find Kate standing outside her building and hadn't been thinking clearly at all. While they rode in silence, Alexi tried to tell herself she'd invited Kate to prove she wasn't as fragile as Kate seemed to think she was. But now, as she replayed the previous day's conversation with Danielle, she wasn't sure. Despite the fact that circumstances were still the same, on some level, Alexi wanted to get to know her better. And given Kate's job that could be dangerous.

But they were in the car and well outside of Nashville so she couldn't do much about it now. Instead she would try to ignore the fact that Kate's hair fell to her shoulder in silken waves and that there was something erotic about the way Kate's slender fingers drummed idly on her knee.

"Did you always want to be a firefighter?" Alexi asked partly out of curiosity and partly to fill the silence with something other than her own thoughts.

Kate nodded. "Never any question."

"Why?"

"There is nothing like walking into a building with fire raging around you. It's the biggest adrenaline rush. But it's so much more than that. We make a difference, whether we're saving lives or someone's property."

"Sounds exciting."

"It was."

"Was?"

"Yeah, when I was on an engine. Now, some days I don't even feel like a firefighter anymore."

"But you still make a difference."

"Maybe." Kate stared out the windshield. "But I guess I grew up with a specific idea of what the job is. My dad and my brother are both firefighters here in Nashville. It's what I wanted for as long as I can remember. But I didn't understand what it really meant until I was in high school and one night our neighbor's house caught on fire. I'll never forget standing outside at three in the morning and watching my father carry two kids, one under each arm, out the front door. The living room flashed over seconds after they got out."

"Wow."

"Yeah. I was so proud of him. I'd been to the station to visit him a ton of times, and by then my brother was already in the academy. But that morning, I really got what it was about."

"How old were you?"

"Fifteen or sixteen."

"That's pretty young to think about risking your life for someone else."

Kate shrugged, surprised that Alexi seemed to understand the seed of fear that had been planted that day. A tiny part of her had wondered if she was really brave enough. At an age when her biggest worry was whether her high-school crush would ask her to the dance that weekend, putting someone else's life first was a lot to grasp. "Any doubts I might have had were erased once I started doing the job."

"So you've never been scared?"

Kate debated lying and wondered if Alexi would believe her. She wasn't supposed to be scared and was certain most of the guys wouldn't have admitted to it. "I have been scared a few times. But it doesn't stop me from doing the job. Besides—" she shrugged—"it's not all hot calls and blazing fires. There are a lot of routine medical calls, smoke alarms, and cats in trees."

"Do you really get cats out of trees?"

"Hey, what can I say? We're all-purpose heroes."

Kate was spared from any further questions when Alexi turned into a winding driveway flanked by stone pillars. Carpets of green lawn stretched back to a cluster of buildings set an acre or so off the road.

"Poplar Springs Rehabilitation Center," Kate read from the painted wooden sign posted at the end of the drive. "Are we visiting someone you know?"

"In a manner of speaking." Alexi eased through the paved circle in front of a sprawling one-story brick building and parked near the entrance.

She led Kate through the automatic doors and into a comfortably decorated lobby. Brightly patterned upholstered chairs were clustered around honey oak coffee tables. Alexi passed through the room and approached a reception desk at the far end.

"Hello, Mrs. Evans," Alexi said to the gray-haired woman behind the counter.

"Miss Alexi, welcome back." The woman smiled warmly. "We missed you last weekend."

"I missed you, too. It's been a crazy week." She nodded at Kate. "This is Kate Chambers, a—friend. Okay if I show her around?"

"Hi there, Kate. Any friend of Alexi's is okay by me. Go on back."

"A friend?" Kate asked when they were out of earshot.

"It was less complicated than the truth."

They entered a large room with thick foam mats and various workout apparatus scattered around. At first Kate thought the room was empty, but in the corner nearest them a man stood with his arms braced on a set of parallel bars. A woman in pale blue scrubs stood in front of him with her hands up as if ready to catch him if he should fall. He inched one leg forward slowly, leaning heavily on the bars. And when he took several painstaking steps, the woman backed up slowly.

"John, you're doing great," Alexi called as she walked over to him.

He looked up and a smile broke the look of concentration on

his face. "Yeah, pretty soon I won't have any more excuses for not dancing with my wife."

"I bet she can't wait." Alexi touched his shoulder. "Keep up the good work."

He put his head back down and resumed his careful progress toward the other end of the bars. Alexi watched for a few more minutes then nodded toward the far end of the room to indicate Kate should follow.

She led Kate through the door at the far end of the room and into a hallway. The doors of several rooms stood open and Kate saw patients of all ages. Some sat up talking to visitors at their bedside or watching television, and others appeared to be sleeping. At the end of the hall they exited into a courtyard. A stone path wide enough to accommodate a wheelchair wound through a well-manicured lawn. A few patients sat with employees soaking up the late-morning sun.

"John was in a motorcycle accident three months ago and his doctor said he probably wouldn't walk." Alexi followed the path around the perimeter of the yard and Kate walked beside her. "He has a ten-year-old daughter. He wants to show her that nothing is impossible."

"That's great."

"He has been working very hard."

They walked on and Kate didn't feel the need to fill the moment of silence. Instead, she listened to the distant chirp of a bird and the soft sound of their sneakers against stone. Alexi's arms swung gently next to Kate's, and Kate could easily imagine that they were just out for a stroll through the park.

"That woman over there under the magnolia tree—she had a stroke and is paralyzed on her left side. For her it's less about getting better and more about learning to cope with her limitations," Alexi said.

"I guess you come here often."

Laughing, Alexi stopped and faced Kate. "Do I come here often? That sounds like a pickup line."

"A bad one." Kate smiled.

A light glimmered in Alexi's eyes, and it struck Kate that this was the first time she'd seen anything resembling happiness on Alexi's face. It seemed all of their conversations were laced with heartache and distrust. Kate stepped closer, wishing she could hold this moment because she suspected it wouldn't last.

Alexi sat on a park bench and leaned her head back, enjoying the warmth of the sun on her face. "I try to make it here at least once a week."

"Why?" Kate settled beside her.

Alexi had already revealed her alcoholism to Kate; certainly the rest should be easier. She inhaled slowly, then shoved aside a flash of panic at revealing too much.

"It took me a long time to admit I had a problem. I used to tell myself I had everything covered. I had a home and a business, and surely if I was an alcoholic I wouldn't be able to maintain those things. I ignored every sign—how I couldn't get through a day without drinking or how on particularly bad ones I couldn't account for whole stretches of time. I rationalized my failed personal relationships and continued to drive away anyone who tried to get close."

"What changed your mind?" Kate turned toward Alexi and stretched her arm along the back of the bench.

"One morning, I woke up in my car outside my apartment with the keys still in the ignition. I went inside and when I turned on the television there was this story about a hit-and-run accident. A woman—a pedestrian—had been struck only a couple of blocks from my place and was in bad shape. The police didn't have any witnesses or leads."

"Oh, Alexi." Kate rubbed a comforting circle against the base of Alexi's neck.

"I ran back outside but I couldn't find a scratch on my car. It wasn't me."

"Thank God," Kate whispered.

"Yes, but that's when it hit me that it very well could have been and I wouldn't even have known it." Alexi remembered the sick feeling in her stomach as she'd inspected her car for signs of an accident. When she hadn't found any damage, she'd vomited right there in the parking lot. That night she'd attended her first Alcoholics Anonymous meeting. "That was when I decided I had to stop drinking."

"And you started volunteering here?"

"Not right away, but yes. I had heard that the woman from the accident ended up here. So after about six months, when I was through the worst of it, I came to visit her. I'm not sure what I would have said to her, but she was gone by that time anyway. But I kept coming back."

"And what happened this week?" Kate's fingers still traced a rhythmic pattern on Alexi's skin.

"I guess I wasn't strong enough, even though I knew how I should be dealing with things—or rather how I shouldn't."

"You said something similar that night at my apartment. But after everything that happened these past several days, you didn't come here and you didn't go to a meeting."

"Even though I knew those were the things that bolstered me? Sounds kind of self-destructive, doesn't it?"

"Is that what you were doing at the Blue Line?"

Was it? "No, not consciously. But there will always be challenges to my sobriety."

"So how can you be certain it won't happen again?"

"I can't."

"That seems like a precarious way to live."

Frustrated, Alexi stood quickly and took a step away. "I don't know, Kate. I don't have all the answers. Do you? Have you decided now that I didn't burn down my own bar? Have you figured out who did? Can you tell me when the insurance company will have your report so I can *finally* move on with my life? Because those are the questions that I need answers to."

"I can't—"

"I didn't think so. I need to take care of a couple of things. I'll find you when I'm ready to go." Without waiting for a response, Alexi strode away. She was aggravated, with Kate but more so with herself. In the past week and a half she'd lost her bar, her personal memories of her father, and her grip on sobriety, and now her life was on hold. The path of her future was in Kate's hands. And despite everything she'd learned in the last year, letting people truly see her was still the one thing Alexi had trouble with.

CHAPTER THIRTEEN

Monday morning, the sun rose in a clear sky and sent its golden rays through the break between the skyscrapers and across Kate's desk. But she barely registered the warmth against the back of her hand as she flipped through a stack of paperwork. She'd awakened early and had been in the office since the first brushes of pink and orange painted the sky. She'd pored over her own case file on the In Left Field fire and now reviewed the file on the fire in the garage. There was no doubt that both fires were the result of arson, and she wasn't content to file them as suspect undetermined.

Leaving her first case unsolved was not how Kate wanted to begin her career as an investigator. She hadn't quite gotten to the point where she was completely okay with her new assignment, but if she was going to do it, then, damn it, she was going to do it well. But no matter how many times she read the report or looked at the photos, she didn't see anything new. They'd already documented all the physical evidence and examined the science of the fire.

She wouldn't find the missing information in these pages, but with Alexi and her partner. Kate was certain they weren't telling her something, and neither of them showed any signs of giving it up. This weekend at the rehab center, Kate had thought she'd made some headway in gaining Alexi's trust. But after

Alexi's outburst, Kate had endured a silent car ride home that put them right back where they were.

Aggravated, she flipped to the beginning of the file and pulled out the photographs again. She was studying them so intently she didn't notice Jason until he was standing next to her desk.

"How many times have you been over that file?" he asked as he peered over her shoulder.

"Too many."

"There won't be anything new in there. If you're not ready to give it up yet, you need to find a break someplace else."

Kate closed the file with an exaggerated gesture. "Like where?"

Jason pulled a chair close and sat down. "When in doubt, follow the money. What about those withdrawals?"

"Alexi said they were business expenses."

Jason raised an eyebrow, which she supposed was because she used Alexi's first name, but he didn't address the personal attachment that it implied. "And you don't believe her?"

"No." That was just one of the many things she sensed Alexi was keeping from her.

"Then talk to her again."

"I don't think she'll tell me anything."

Jason shrugged and smoothed two fingers over his mustache. "I'm ready to file this as suspect unknown. So if you're not, you need to bring me something new. Do you have anything else?"

"No."

"Then get her to tell you the truth or we're done with this." Jason pulled open the top drawer of her desk and lifted out her navy necktie. "But first, put this on. And go get your dress blazer." He stood and buttoned the top button of his shirt.

"Where are we going?"

"I have to go to court and I want you to come with me."

Kate retrieved her jacket, and when she returned Jason was knotting his own tie. He handed her a file, then shrugged on his jacket.

The A. A. Birch Building occupied most of the block south of the fire marshal's office and was visible as soon as they stepped outside. The new courthouse, with its smooth white stone exterior and contrasting blue mirror-tinted windows, had been completed the year before and now housed both the criminal and civil courts for Davidson County.

"This is an attempted-murder case. A man beat his wife until she was unconscious, then set their house on fire and left. She suffered from smoke inhalation, broken bones, and some pretty severe burns."

"That's horrible." As they crossed the street, Kate opened the file and glanced at the photos of the scene. There were also pictures of the woman's injuries, apparently taken at the hospital immediately after the fire. She couldn't imagine a jury looking at them and not putting the guy in jail.

"From what I understand, the couple has a long history of abuse but she's never been willing to press charges. The police have tried a few times, but without her cooperation, he's never gotten more than a slap on the wrist. She's finally ready to prosecute."

Kate and Jason fell in with a stream of people headed into the courthouse. Men and women in suits escorted nervous-looking clients. Police officers nodded at Kate, a gesture of professional recognition that she returned.

"Usually, you'll meet with whichever assistant district attorney is handling the case at least once before the court date to go over your testimony." Jason moved into line behind a couple of officers waiting to pass through the metal detector. As with the officers in front of them, Jason and Kate were waved through by the security guard. "It's usually pretty straightforward. The ADA will lead you with their questions. Since most of our testimony is based on proven science the defense won't have much to refute, but they'll also get their opportunity to question you."

They took the elevator up to the sixth floor, then exited into a long hallway. Jason continued to the end of the hall, passing several doors labeled with the name of whichever judge presided in that division.

"Have a seat. We wait out here." Jason indicated a row of benches that resembled church pews, situated against the wall.

On one bench a group of people seemed to be closing ranks around the woman seated in the center. Compression garments covered both of her arms, and a scar constricted the skin on one side of her neck and jaw before it disappeared into the high neck of her shirt. She sat silently, her eyes downcast and her purse resting in her lap. Two women flanked her, one older and one younger, and though neither of them touched her, they angled toward her protectively.

Kate chose an empty bench closest to the courtroom doors. "How long do we sit here?"

"Until we're called. We can't hear the statements of any of the other witnesses before we testify. Each attorney will give his opening statement, then the prosecutor will start presenting his case. We'll be called as one of his witnesses."

"Do you have any pointers on testifying?"

"Answer only the question you're asked, don't volunteer extra information. Look at the jury when you answer. You're a firefighter, so they already want to trust you. Make eye contact, don't look around too much or fidget in the chair. Show them you're calm and confident in what you're saying and they'll take everything you say as the gospel."

Nearly an hour later, the door opened and a man stepped into the hallway and called Jason's name. Kate followed him inside and slipped into a row near the back of the courtroom. Rows of the same dark pews filled the first half of the large room, separated from the rest of the room by a low wooden barrier.

Jason continued toward the front of the room. He stopped a few feet from the judge's bench and turned to the clerk seated to the left and a step below the judge. He raised his right hand and waited while she read an oath, then answered affirmatively. Kate watched carefully as she would have to complete these same steps herself someday. Jason projected an air of confidence and his movements were controlled and deliberate. He stepped into the witness box, unbuttoned his jacket, and sat down.

A man Kate assumed was the ADA stood and moved behind a podium situated between two long tables that faced the judge's bench. He didn't look old enough to be out of college, let alone law school. He stood a little too quickly and reached up to nervously adjust his tie so often that his gesture was distracting.

He adjusted the microphone to his height, flinching at the creaking noise as he bent it down, then asked Jason to state his name and occupation. Referring often to the open file in front of him, he questioned Jason about his investigation of the house fire. As Jason had predicted, most of the questions were straightforward and could be answered by referencing the incident reports the investigators had filled out at the time of the fire.

When the ADA finished, the defense attorney took a turn. Kate couldn't help but compare the two lawyers. The defense attorney was the picture of confidence as he smoothed a hand over his rust-colored tie. The color was a bold choice, but with his trendy haircut and stylish square-rimmed glasses, he pulled it off. He asked only a few follow-up questions before Jason was released. Jason came back and slid onto the bench next to her.

"Aren't we done?" Alexi whispered while the next witness was being summoned.

"Usually, yes. But I want you to hear this." Jason nodded toward the woman from the hallway as she noticeably limped up the center aisle to the front of the courtroom.

After she was sworn in, the woman took her place in the witness box. She glanced at the jury then away, and her hand hovered self-consciously at her neck.

From the beginning, it was painful to watch her testimony. The prosecutor was obviously careful with his questions, but still she was unable to contain her tears and the occasional sob as she talked about their tumultuous relationship, punctuated with his drinking and frequent accusations of her infidelity.

When she began to describe the events of that night, she began to cry in earnest, and the judge called a short recess to allow her to compose herself. Minutes later, she returned to the stand, looking no more composed. Now she clutched a tissue in her fist and her hands shook as she sat back down.

"Mrs. Hertz, I understand this is difficult, but I need you to tell me what happened on the evening of June fourteenth this year. What time did your husband get home that night?"

"Shortly after seven."

"And how would you describe his mood?"

"He was angry about something that happened at work." Her voice shook and she cleared her throat before she continued. "When I asked him why he was letting it upset him, he yelled at me. He said I was too stupid to understand his job." She looked down at her lap as she said the last part, as if embarrassed to admit her husband's insult.

She seemed to be trying very hard not to look at her husband, but he was having no such problem. Seated next to his attorney at a table along the left wall of the courtroom, he had a direct view of the witness box, and when he angled his body to watch his wife, Kate was able to study him. Outwardly he appeared respectful, dressed in a suit and tie, with his hands tucked beneath the table. But his eyes never left his wife, and Kate wondered if the jury could see the predatory gleam in them. Surely they could, since she could spot it from the back of the room. His shoulders bunched as if he were wringing his hands together under the table. The tension of holding himself back radiated from his stiff posture and clenched jaw.

Kate turned her attention to the jury as the woman described her husband's escalating anger. Some of them looked at her and others stared at their laps, apparently uncomfortable with her pain. Every so often a pair of eyes flickered to her husband and lingered for just a moment before returning to her.

"Then he hit me in the face," Mrs. Hertz said quickly, as if she were having to force the words out.

"With his fist or an open hand?"

Her eyebrows drew together as she struggled to remember the painful memory. "With the back of his hand, I think."

"Did he strike you more than once?"

She nodded.

"Mrs. Hertz, I need you to answer aloud, for the court record."

"Yes."

"What happened after Mr. Hertz hit you?"

"I fell backward, into the table, and before I could get up he was there—hitting me again and again. I couldn't see because there was blood in my eyes, but he yelled at me the entire time."

"What did he say?"

"Mostly he just called me names."

"Mrs. Hertz, I know this is difficult, but I need you to tell me specifically what he called you."

She nodded and took a deep breath. For a long moment the only sound in the courtroom was the creak of jurors fidgeting in their chairs.

"He called me a—stupid slut. He said it was all my fault for being such a bitch." Her face and neck flushed and her voice shook as she said the words. "That I made him so angry he couldn't help himself and that I deserved a lot worse than what I was getting."

"What happened next?"

"I'm sorry, but that's all I can remember. The next thing I knew, I woke up alone and the house was on fire."

"He was gone?"

"Yes."

"And what condition did you awaken in?"

"Um, my left eye was swollen shut, and when I tried to move, everything hurt. There was so much smoke, the fire was so close, I could feel it on my skin but I couldn't—"

She stumbled, her voice choked with emotion. The prosecutor waited patiently but silently. Kate glanced at the jury and found all eyes on the woman on the witness stand. Like at an accident scene, none of them could pull their gaze from her as she broke down. She smoothed out the tissue she'd been clutching so tight, then swiped it across her cheek.

"I'm sorry," she murmured.

"It's okay." The prosecutor lifted a folder from the table nearby. "Your Honor, while Mrs. Hertz collects herself, I would like to offer these photographs, taken by the police that night at the hospital." Once more the evidence was handed to the court officer. Kate knew the photos portrayed the gruesome scene better than Mrs. Hertz could with mere words.

When it seemed Mrs. Hertz had sufficiently gathered her composure, the prosecutor began to question her again.

"Were you able to get out of the house on your own?"

She shook her head. "No," she said quickly, glancing at the court reporter in apology. "I couldn't see very well, and I couldn't move. It seemed like forever until the firemen got to me and they carried me out."

"Were you taken to the hospital?"

"Yes."

"And what was the extent of your injuries?"

"My right leg was broken. I had four fractured ribs and burns over my arms, chest, and neck. I also had multiple facial fractures."

Kate watched Mr. Hertz's face as his wife described her injuries and saw no trace of remorse. In fact, she saw the tug of a smug smile at the corner of his lips. But when he glanced at his attorney, the lawyer gave an almost imperceptible shake of his head and Mr. Hertz's expression became neutral.

"I have nothing further for this witness."

Kate had been so intent on Mr. Hertz's reaction that she'd missed the prosecutor's remaining question.

Mr. Hertz's attorney stood and stepped to the podium. He began with an expression of sympathy for the woman's injuries, then asked her a series of specific questions about the night of the fire. Most of them she'd already answered, and Kate thought he might just be asking them to upset her. He asked if she had ever been unfaithful to her husband and when she answered no, he asked if she was certain. He talked about a pregnancy she'd ended and forced her to admit that she had lied and told her husband she had miscarried. But Kate wasn't sure if he lost or gained points when she said that she couldn't stomach the idea of watching him abuse their child. She felt it would be cruel to bring a child into their home when she already knew of its painful fate. He peppered her with questions for another thirty minutes, obviously attempting to portray her as dishonest and thus discredit her earlier statements.

After her testimony, the judge called another recess. Jason touched Kate's elbow to indicate they should go and she followed him out.

"What do you think?" he asked after they rode the elevator down and exited the building.

"I think she should have gotten out of her marriage earlier." As they started up the sidewalk toward the office, a gust of wind swept a strand of Kate's hair free from her bun and she tucked it behind her ear.

"Yes, but aside from that?"

"Well, if he really did it, that's pretty horrible."

"Oh, he did it. The evidence they're going to hand the jury is overwhelming. And regardless of what history led them to that point, what he did to her was inhuman."

Kate nodded. "So this was about more than just showing me the process for testifying."

"You needed to know all of that too. But I also wanted you to see this case specifically. I can't offer you the excitement of an active fire or the adrenaline rush. But our testimony today will help put that man away for a long time, and that is no less important than the actions of those firefighters who pulled her out of the house, because if he doesn't go to prison, he *will* kill her eventually. This job *does* matter, Kate. It may not feel like it when we're writing reports or issuing citations for burn-permit violations. But we can make a difference. It's just not as glamorous, and we don't get to wear turnout gear anymore."

"Or pose for the calendar in our suspenders," Kate joked.

"Oh, I don't know." Jason squeezed her bicep. "If you stay in shape, for you, they just might make an exception."

❖

"Scotch, neat, please."

Alexi grabbed a glass and began to make the drink even before she looked up at her customer. When she did she immediately stopped pouring. Anthony Wilde slid onto a stool at the bar opposite her.

"Hello, Ms. Clark, it's good to see you again."

"Mr. Wilde, what are you doing here?" Alexi debated how much trouble she'd get in if she refused to serve him. But her boss hadn't yet forgiven her for the scene she'd created three nights ago, so she decided not to push her luck.

"I came to see you."

"You didn't send one of your associates?" She set a glass in front of him.

He shrugged. "I figured you'd just throw him out."

"Probably."

"I've been looking for Ronnie and he's making himself scarce, so I hoped you would get a message to him."

"I'm not one of your errand boys." Alexi busied herself

filling an order for a waiting server. She set three draft beers on a tray and added an order of hot wings from the kitchen.

"Mr. Volk and I have some business to settle and he seems to be avoiding my calls."

"Well, what are you planning to do? We don't have anything left to burn down."

He scowled and leaned forward. When he spoke his voice was low and menacing. "As I told you before, neither myself nor anyone acting on my behalf had anything to do with the damage to your property, and I would appreciate it if you would not suggest that we did."

"Even if I believed—"

"I promise you, Ms. Clark, you don't want to spread such blatant lies about me."

Alexi pressed her palms to the bar and met his eyes. "I don't appreciate being threatened."

He sat back and raised his hands. "No threats here. I simply don't wish to have you smearing my reputation."

Alexi nearly laughed. It wasn't as if his reputation was sterling to begin with.

He pushed his empty glass across the bar and gestured for a refill. "Since you're so concerned about the truth, maybe you should ask your partner where he was the night of the fire."

"He was at home with his wife." Alexi shook a martini and poured it into a glass, then served it to a customer two stools down from Anthony.

"Are you sure?"

"Yes."

"Was that after he left my place?"

In the midst of pouring another row of shots, Alexi paused. When liquid spilled over the edge of a glass, she fumbled to right the bottle quickly. "What are you talking about?"

"He came into my bar to pay me his weekly installment just before one a.m. Had the nerve to ask for some action on the Duke game. I told him I was through with him. I thought he had left, but about an hour later, on my way out, I saw him drinking at the bar with some of the guys."

Alexi stared at him.

"Tell your partner to call me." Anthony dropped a twenty on the bar and walked away.

Should she believe him? Would he lie to cause problems for Ron? They obviously weren't on the best of terms. He'd met her eyes and stated things so matter-of-factly that Alexi hadn't gotten the impression what he said was a lie. But then again, he might just be adept at deception. She wouldn't jump to any conclusions until after she talked to Ron.

Chapter Fourteen

How are you holding up, sweetie?"

"I'm okay." Alexi wasn't surprised to find Danielle on her doorstep on Tuesday morning. She'd been calling several times a day since Alexi admitted she'd had a lapse. Last night, her phone hadn't stopped ringing while she was working, so she had finally turned it off. This morning she'd been awakened by the doorbell and thrown on her flannel robe to answer the door, already knowing who stood on the other side.

"Good, because I called your cell last night and you didn't answer, so I thought something might be wrong."

"Nope. I'm all good—clean and sober. We were just super busy and I couldn't talk." Alexi turned and headed for the kitchen, leaving the door open. "Come on in. I was just about to start the coffee."

"If you wanted me to leave you alone, all you had to do was say so."

Alexi couldn't come up with a correct response to that statement, so she ignored it. If she had told Danielle she wanted her to stop calling, it would have hurt her feelings more than not answering the phone had. She'd learned long ago that when dealing with Danielle it was easier to apologize later.

"You know I worry about you. I hate that all that's going on has caused you to drink again."

Alexi paused, took a deep breath, then resumed measuring the coffee. "It was a minor setback, Danielle. It won't happen again."

"Good."

"Anthony Wilde visited the Blue Line last night."

"Really? What did he want?"

"He was looking for Ron. He also told me that Ron wasn't at home with you on the night of the fire." Alexi rested her hip against the counter and watched Danielle for a reaction. She was disappointed by the slight tightening around Danielle's mouth. "Why would he say that? Is it true?"

Danielle shook her head slowly, but the tears welling in her eyes betrayed her.

"Oh, Danielle."

"Ron figured they would suspect him so he asked me to say he was there."

"I understand how you could deceive the investigators, though I don't condone it. But you looked me in the eye and lied. To *me*."

"I'm so sorry." A tear spilled down Danielle's cheek and she rubbed it away.

"Damn it." Alexi pulled a tissue from a box on the counter and handed it to Danielle. Her head swam with this new information. "Where was he?"

"Does it matter?"

"Yes, it does. Especially if he was setting my bar on fire." She'd thought since the beginning the fire might be connected to Ron. But her theory had involved someone trying to send him a message. She hadn't thought Ron could have actually set the fire himself.

"He wasn't."

"You're sure?"

"Yes." Danielle avoided eye contact. Instead, she turned away and took two mugs from the cabinet. She pulled the carafe out and held a mug beneath the stream coming from the coffeemaker, then handed it to Alexi.

"Then where was he?"

"He never came home after you told him to leave early. He said he went out for drinks with some friends."

"Why didn't he just tell them he was at Tony's?"

"If they started asking questions over there, they might dig up his gambling debt."

"So? If it's not connected to the fire, what difference does it make?"

"He didn't want anyone to know. He prides himself on the success of the bar and hated that he had to take money to pay his debts."

Alexi abandoned her coffee on the counter. "So his damn reputation was more important than our business."

"Alexi, you don't understand."

"I don't understand? You don't think I know how it feels to have your reputation shot to hell by your own actions—to have everything you do called into question because of your past mistakes?"

"And you also know that it can take a long time to admit you need help. And that in the meantime you can cause a lot of hurt." Danielle's tone was heavily laced with accusation.

"It always comes back to that, doesn't it?" Alexi didn't expect an answer. "What time did he get home?"

"He says he slept in the car."

"Why didn't he call you to come get him?"

"I don't know. We've been having problems. Maybe he didn't want to come home."

"Then how can you be so sure he didn't set the fire?"

"He doesn't have it in him." Danielle's voice carried a hint of disdain. But before Alexi could question it, she went on. "I'll admit he's never loved the place like you did. But then again, who could?"

"What does that mean?"

"Come on, Alexi. That place was your whole life. There was no room for anything or anyone else."

Anger trickled into Alexi's blood. Ron and Danielle had deceived her in order to cover his own problems, and now Danielle was attacking her priorities. "That's ridiculous."

"You're right. Who can say what caused your relationship problems. Between your complete obsession with the bar and your being a drunk, I mean."

Alexi's anger turned to a hot flood, flashing through her. "I can't believe you just said that."

"You have no right to judge Ron. He's trying to protect us. All of us. That's more than I can say about you."

She'd been selfish before. She could admit that, and had, more than once. But how long did she have to keep paying for past sins? Could she ever redeem herself for the mistakes she'd made while she was drinking? Or would they forever be the ghosts that Danielle and Ron resurrected and used against her on a whim?

"I think you should go."

"Alexi—"

"Unless the next words out of your mouth are an apology, I really don't want to talk about this anymore right now."

Danielle nodded and set her jaw in a stubborn gesture Alexi was used to seeing. As she left, Alexi stayed in the kitchen until she heard the quiet click of the door closing.

❖

"Did you forget something?" Alexi asked as she opened the door again five minutes later. But it wasn't Danielle on the other side. Instead she came face-to-face with Kate. "Sorry. I thought you were someone else."

"Apparently." Kate's eyes swept downward. Alexi flushed and pulled her robe tighter around her. "Can I come in?"

Alexi wondered if she imagined the slight huskiness in Kate's voice. She stepped back and made room for Kate to enter. "There's coffee in the kitchen. Help yourself while I go put something else on."

"Thank you."

Kate disappeared into the kitchen and Alexi fled to her bedroom. Once there she shed her robe and pulled on a pair of blue jeans and a T-shirt. She glanced down to assess her appearance and could easily make out the firm peaks of her nipples beneath the thin cotton.

"Damn it," she muttered as she grabbed a cable-knit sweater and jerked it over her head. She detoured to the bathroom and checked her reflection in the mirror. *Not bad, if you like the exhausted look.* She smoothed a hand over her hair and down the side of her neck and debated whether she should add some concealer to the dark crescents under her eyes. What was she worried about anyway? Despite the heat Alexi had seen in her eyes as she looked her over, Kate was most likely not here to make a social call.

When she returned to the kitchen, Kate handed her a cup of coffee. Kate held the handle of the mug until Alexi had a good grip on it, their fingers nearly entwined in the transfer.

"Be careful, it's hot." Kate pulled her hand away slowly, brushing the back of Alexi's hand.

Alexi searched Kate's face, looking for a sign that the contact was deliberate, but she found nothing. Kate seemed completely unaware that the light touch had made Alexi shiver. Alexi turned away under the ruse of adding cream to her coffee.

"What can I do for you, Ms. Chambers?"

"You can fill in some details that I'm still missing."

"I'm not sure there's anything else I can tell you."

"Why don't you let me be the judge of that?"

"Let's sit." Trying to appear more composed than she felt, Alexi led Kate to the living room. Alexi bypassed the sofa and sat in the chair nearby.

"I wanted to ask you again about the withdrawals from your account."

"I told you—"

"I know, they were business expenses." Kate set her mug on a coaster on the table in front of her. She leaned forward and met Alexi's eyes. "Now I need to know the real reason for those transactions."

Danielle's words echoed in Alexi's head. Danielle and Ron had both conspired to alibi each other and left her out on her own. And even when they knew she was stressing about being a suspect, neither of them had confessed the truth to her. Why was she trying to protect Ron's reputation? She'd wanted to track down the origin of the fire on her own, but in truth she'd had no idea how to go about it. So why shouldn't she help the investigators do their job? More importantly, why shouldn't she help Kate?

"Ron withdrew the money." Alexi felt a rush of panic as soon as she admitted the truth.

"What did he use it for?"

"He didn't have anything to do with the fire."

"Alexi, what was the money for?"

"He had a debt to pay."

"I've seen the amounts. That's a lot of debt."

Alexi hesitated. Maybe she shouldn't be telling Kate about this. She didn't need Kate. She could still figure this out on her own.

"Okay. That much money," Kate said as if she were thinking aloud. "Financial problems, bad investments, gambling." Alexi couldn't keep from flinching when Kate said "gambling" and she knew Kate saw her reaction. "I guess we have a winner."

"Kate—"

"You should have told me."

"Is it really relevant?"

"How could I know unless you told me? I asked you if

anyone had a grudge against either of you. I would say owing that kind of money could inspire some bitterness."

"No. I talked to Anthony Wilde and I don't think he had anything to do with the fire."

"Anthony Wilde?"

"I guess you'd call him Ron's bookie."

Kate stared at Alexi, not believing what she was hearing. "You went to see Ron's bookie? By yourself?"

"Yes. But like I said, I don't think he was involved."

"And what if he was? Didn't you realize the guy could be dangerous? Are you an idiot?" Kate fired off her questions without waiting for an answer. She was probably being harsh, but the idea that Alexi could have been in danger scared her more than anything had in some time.

"What? No, of course I'm not an idiot."

"You could have been hurt."

"Obviously, I wasn't. And I can take care of myself."

"But you don't have to." Kate surged to her feet in anger. When she realized how telling her words were, she added, "You should have let Jason and me do our jobs." She walked around the sofa, needing the movement in order to collect her thoughts. Ron Volk had a gambling problem. Now she had that new lead she was looking for—a thread to follow that might direct the investigation away from Alexi.

"I thought your job was to prove I was guilty." Alexi stood and rounded the other end of the sofa. Kate changed direction and paced away from her.

"My job is to determine if the fire was the result of arson and find the suspect."

"And I am one of your suspects."

"We needed to look at every possible—"

"Just say it, Kate."

When Kate turned around, Alexi stood right in front of her. Too close. She looked down, mostly to avoid the accusation in

Alexi's eyes. Alexi's sock-clad toes were just inches from the tips of Kate's shoes, and, though she knew it was ridiculous, Kate imagined for a moment that she could feel them—a teasing nudge across the couch on a Sunday morning. *What?* What the hell was she doing thinking about Sunday mornings?

"I need to hear it."

Kate dragged her eyes back up to Alexi's and saw the disappointment shadowing them. She couldn't say it. Because, though she no longer believed Alexi had set those fires, her certainty wasn't entirely professional. So instead she changed the subject. "I need an address for Anthony Wilde."

"You can find him at Tony's on Demonbruen Street," Alexi snapped. "See how easy it is to answer a question when you're asked?"

"Alexi."

"Tell me that you think I'm capable of burning down my own bar."

"We shouldn't—"

"Say it."

"Damn it, Alexi." Kate grabbed Alexi's shoulders, jerked her close, and kissed her. Hard. She was aggressive, without apology, sweeping her tongue inside Alexi's mouth. And when they separated, they were both breathing hard. Kate still clutched Alexi's shoulders and she rested her forehead against Alexi's. "Just shut up, okay?"

Kate stroked her hands down the outside of Alexi's arms to her waist. Alexi sighed and Kate felt the whispered breath against her face. Alexi slipped her hands into Kate's hair and urged her closer. This kiss was gentler and unhurried. Alexi's lips were soft and responsive, and Kate lost her head for a long moment.

Almost against her will, Kate eased back. "This is a very, very bad idea." Arousal spread through her like warm honey, slow and sweet. She curled her fingers around the waistband of Alexi's jeans, clutching denim and the wide leather of her belt.

"Yes. It is."

Kate tugged experimentally and Alexi's hips tilted closer. "We should stop."

Alexi slowly pulled her hands from Kate's hair, letting them trail over Kate's jaw. "You're right."

"I'll go." Kate didn't move.

"You don't have to." Alexi's fingers lingered at the base of Kate's throat, playing lightly against her skin.

Alexi's voice was saturated with innuendo that made Kate's heart race and her knees actually feel weak. Well, really it was her whole legs and they were more numb than weak, but regardless, she'd never thought that kind of thing happened in real life.

"If I stay—well, I just don't think that would be a smart thing for either of us." Kate didn't want to leave. She wanted to stand here with Alexi pressed against her for a little while longer and see where these feelings took them. But even if she forgot that she was supposed to be working today, could she simply shove aside the argument they'd just had? Or the fact that Alexi was involved in one of her cases?

"Ah, well, apparently I'm an idiot and I do stupid things," Alexi said with a small smile.

"With you, I could be convinced to do stupid things." Alexi looked shocked at Kate's words, but she was no more surprised than Kate was that she'd actually spoken her thoughts out loud. Kate jerked back a step, because it seemed the best way to separate herself from Alexi and whatever spell had stolen her inhibitions. "I have to go."

"Wait." Alexi took several steps forward, but Kate matched them and kept the distance between them.

"I didn't mean to say that. This can't happen." Kate backed toward the door. "Promise me if you get any more information about the fire you'll call me."

"Is that what this was about?"

"No. But I don't think you should be running around out there investigating on your own."

"Thank you for your concern. But my safety isn't your

responsibility." Alexi reached around Kate and opened the door. "Good-bye, Ms. Chambers."

Chapter Fifteen

Ron Volk has a gambling problem," Kate announced as she walked into the office that afternoon.

"Really? How did you figure that out?" Jason looked up from his computer.

"I did what you told me. I talked to Alexi Clark."

He nodded. "Good. Do we know where he placed his bets?"

Kate sat at her desk and started up her computer. "A place on Demonbruen. Tony's."

"Kind of a rough crowd down there. I can't picture Ron Volk hanging out there. He seems to think he's a better class of people than he actually is."

"He does think a lot of himself." Kate pulled up her search engine and typed in Anthony Wilde's name.

Jason walked around to her desk and looked over her shoulder as she scanned the results. "So Ms. Clark thinks Wilde had something to do with the fire?"

"No, actually, she doesn't. Apparently, she's already been to see him."

"Why didn't she tell us about this?"

Kate shrugged. "Don't ask me to explain anything that woman does."

"Whoa, I'm sensing some tension. Did something happen that I need to know about?"

"You mean other than the fact that she's apparently been running around asking questions behind our backs instead of helping us?"

"It's not uncommon for people to be uncooperative in our investigations, especially when they know they might be suspects." Jason straightened and returned to his desk.

"But she's not still a suspect, is she?"

"What do you think?"

"The two fires have got to be connected, so we can assume we're looking for one suspect. Even if I could believe she started the bar fire, I don't believe Alexi could have set the fire in the garage. That car meant too much to her."

"And the evidence?"

"Nothing points to her that can't be explained by the fact that she owns the property, other than her not having an alibi."

"So her sentimentality about her father's belongings is your reason for excluding her? Is it possible she just has you completely snowed?"

Kate considered the question. Was Alexi conning her? Could she be letting her attraction to Alexi cloud her judgment? Kate didn't think the grief she'd seen in the alley the day of the garage fire was contrived. And perhaps she'd crossed a line personally with Alexi, but she also believed the anguish in Alexi's hazy eyes that night in the bar was genuine as well. "My gut tells me she wasn't involved. And we haven't found any real evidence to contradict that feeling."

"I agree."

"You do? Then what was all of that about?"

"Just a bit of devil's advocate." Jason grabbed his coat from the back of his chair. "Let's go talk to the bookie."

❖

"We're here to see Anthony Wilde," Jason said as he strode directly to the bar.

"He ain't seeing no visitors," the bartender grunted, without looking away from the television behind the bar.

"He'll want to talk to us."

"Who's asking?"

"Arson investigators. We're with the Nashville Fire Department."

The bartender finally looked at Jason, his eyes dropping down then traveling back up. If he was assessing his chances against Jason, they were slim. Jason towered over him by nearly six inches, and Jason's bulk was in muscle whereas his centered around his middle.

"Just a minute." He picked up the phone.

While they waited, Kate looked around. The room was dimly lit, but the shadows failed to hide the scarred tables and damaged wood floor. The dark walls were decorated with autographed photos of athletes, but Kate didn't recognize any of them. She couldn't imagine that this place provided much competition for Alexi's bar. The pool table appeared decades older than those she'd seen in photos of Alexi's place, and the dartboard on the far wall looked like it would fall down if someone actually threw a dart at it.

At the far end of the bar an over-processed blonde draped against a man with a gray ponytail and a leather vest. Their exposed arms were covered in tattoos, and a line of piercings that ran up the woman's earlobe and kept on going.

"I see what you meant by rough crowd," Kate said quietly. A group of men crowded around several of the tables closest to the television and watched a college basketball game. The score was apparently close, and as the lead changed quickly back and forth, different guys cheered for their respective team.

"May I help you?" a gravelly voice asked from the doorway behind them.

When Jason and Alexi turned, Anthony Wilde stepped out of

the office instead of inviting them in. He closed the door behind him and crossed his arms. Kate could already guess how this interview would go.

"I'm Jason Hayworth and this is Kate Chambers. We're here to ask you a few questions about a fire at the establishment of one of your competitors."

"If this is about In Left Field, I've already told Ms. Clark more than once that I don't know anything about it. And now she's sent you to do her bidding. I've got to say, this is bordering on harassment. Is the city condoning that now?"

"No one has sent us. We're simply gathering information on an active case. There's no need to get defensive." Jason remained composed despite Anthony's hostile tone.

"My tax dollars at work," Anthony grumbled.

"The sooner you cooperate, the sooner we can get out of here."

Kate looked around, letting her distaste show in her expression. "And believe me, we don't want to hang around any longer than we have to."

"You should watch your mouth, young lady."

"Let's focus on the matter at hand," Jason said. "We understand that Ron Volk owes you a sizable gambling debt."

"Mr. Hayworth, gambling is illegal, and I can assure you—"

"We're not police officers, Mr. Wilde. I don't care what you have going on here. At least, I won't as long as you answer our questions. I'm only trying to determine if that debt might have something to do with the fire."

"That's not how I do business."

"What about Ron Volk? In your opinion, would he be capable of setting the fire in order to get the insurance money?"

"Ronnie? Hell, no. He doesn't have the balls for it. His wife has got his in a jar."

"Thank you for your time, Mr. Wilde." Jason scanned the

bar one last time, then nodded to Kate to signal that they were leaving.

They walked outside and went immediately to Jason's Tahoe parked near the door.

"What do you think?" Kate asked after she was situated in the passenger seat.

"That guy is small-time. He's not nearly as important as he thinks he is." Jason slid behind the wheel.

"I agree. And I think he's right about Ron Volk."

Ron didn't strike Kate as a risk taker. She got the impression that the bar was Alexi's idea and Ron had seen a chance to jump on board as an investor. He didn't have the passion for the place that Alexi had. What exactly that meant for the future of Ron and Alexi's partnership, Kate didn't know.

"You've been spending more time hanging around this station than you did when you worked here."

"I'm hoping for a contact high," Kate said as she walked into the kitchen. There was more truth in her flippant words than she cared to admit. The familiar sights and sounds of the fire station made her feel at home. If she told anyone that the smells of stale smoke from the turnout gear hanging in the truck bay or the hint of exhaust as she passed the trucks inspired feelings of security, they would probably think she was crazy. But it was true.

Paula, the room's lone occupant, stood by the stove stirring the contents of a large pot. Kate had passed the guys from the engine removing hose from the hose dryer on the way in. And Paula's partner was on the phone in the next room.

Paula laughed. "Are things getting any better with the new job?"

"I guess so. It's not like riding an engine, but it's not as bad as I originally thought."

"You'll just have to get your excitement somewhere else, huh?"

Kate nodded. "Speaking of which, are you making any progress with Dr. Fields?"

"I think so. We've taken several patients to her hospital lately."

"Is she warming up to you?"

"She's still playing hard to get." Paula grinned. "But there's something in her eyes when we go in there. I think she may actually be happy to see me. And last time I asked her out for coffee, I believe she thought about it for a minute before she said no."

"Persistence pays off."

"Maybe. But I'm kind of enjoying just flirting with her. She's smart and quick-witted. I never thought *not* dating someone could be so much fun."

"It's different, letting her set the pace, isn't it?"

"Different. Maddening. Arousing."

Kate laughed. "You've just summed up women in three words."

"What about you? Anything new with that woman from the bar?"

"Alexi? That's strictly professional."

"Really? Because it didn't look very professional when you were half carrying her out of the bar."

"She'd been drinking. I was trying to keep her from picking a fight with her boss."

"Let me ask you something, did you take her home?"

"Well, yes. But I wasn't sure she could get there safely by herself."

Paula nodded and dipped a spoon into the pot. "Here, taste."

"That's good. What is it?"

"Stew. Bear brought in some venison." Paula took another

spoonful for herself, then added salt and pepper. "So, you escorted her safely to her door. Then what?"

"Actually, I took her to my place." Knowing how that sounded, Kate winced. But without revealing Alexi's alcoholism, she couldn't explain why she hadn't felt right simply dropping Alexi off at her apartment. And while she trusted Paula, she still felt like she would be betraying Alexi's confidence to do so.

"Ah, that's keeping it professional. Did you sleep with her?"

"No," Kate answered quickly.

"But you want to."

Kate debated lying, but given Paula's piercing look there was no need. "Yes. But she's connected to a case."

"Is she a suspect?"

"Not anymore."

Paula raised an eyebrow indicating she wanted to know more, but was wise enough not to ask the specifics of an investigation. "Is the case closed?"

"It will be. If we don't get a break soon."

"Is there some kind of statute of limitations? You know, after so long is it okay to go out with her?"

"I don't know, Paula. I've never been in this situation before. When I think about it, it seems like it should be crossing a line, but when I'm with her, the lines get blurry. Though there's something about her. I can't get her out of my head."

"It sounds like you need to figure out this case first. Then maybe you'll know what to do about the girl."

Figure out the case first. An hour later, when Kate got out of her Tahoe in front of the Blue Line, she told herself that was exactly what she intended to do. The parking lot was unusually full for early evening, and several other people arrived while

Kate was loitering outside. A group of men climbed out of a car, talking and laughing. They all had military-style haircuts and walked with a distinct swagger. Kate followed them inside, and when they paused to accept greetings from those already there, she slid past them and picked her way through the crowd.

Behind the bar, Alexi and another bartender hurried to keep up with the incoming orders. Kate found an empty stool near Alexi's end of the counter.

"Beer?" Alexi asked, sparing Kate barely a glance.

Kate nodded.

When Alexi returned a minute later with an open bottle, Kate said, "I didn't expect you to be so busy."

"The police academy graduated a class this afternoon."

Kate nodded and Alexi moved away to help a new customer three stools down from Kate. As she nursed her beer, Kate watched Alexi work. She really was a good bartender, and Kate could imagine that she had been a good bar manager as well. She filled orders quickly but still took the time to make small talk with regulars and smile at new customers.

One of the academy graduates sidled up to the bar, and Kate could tell by his body language that he was trying to flirt with Alexi while she made his drink. Alexi slid the glass across the bar and rebuffed him politely. He returned to his table and faced the none-too-gentle ribbing from his friends at his failed conquest. One of the other men stood and looked over at Alexi. He tugged at his collar and said something to his compatriots that elicited a round of laughter. He strutted to the bar amid catcalls from his buddies.

When he leaned across the bar and spoke to Alexi, the intimate gesture caused a knot in Kate's stomach. She forced herself to stay rooted on her stool even when the man reached out and caught Alexi's wrist as she passed a beer to him. When Alexi tried to jerk her hand away, the man held on and Kate surged to her feet.

She was behind him in seconds, soon enough to hear Alexi's

polite attempt to regain control of the situation and his obvious disregard.

"I think she wants you to let go of her." Without thinking, Kate grabbed his forearm and immediately felt the cords of muscle there stiffen. Alexi winced as his hand tightened around her wrist.

He glanced over his shoulder at Kate and sneered. "Are you jealous? Because there's enough of me to go around, baby."

He was several inches taller than Kate and she couldn't even guess by how much he outweighed her. The hard muscles beneath her hand and the large, defined bulk of his shoulders told Kate she would probably lose this fight. But he still held Alexi captive, so Kate didn't consider backing down. "I said, leave her alone."

He released Alexi's wrist, but when Kate's attention swung to Alexi, he circled his hand around Kate's upper arm. "I guess you want me all to yourself then."

"Actually, I don't want you at all."

Kate was plotting the projectile of her knee into his groin when Alexi interrupted.

"Take your beer, on the house, and go rejoin your friends. We can pretend this never happened. Otherwise, I'll have you thrown out of here on your ass." She nodded toward the other bartender, who was a much better physical match for him.

By now, the crowd around them was watching. He glanced at them and flushed. But in the end, he relented. He picked up his beer and slinked away.

Kate barely registered the jeers that greeted him across the room. She kept her eyes on Alexi, who stood behind the bar rubbing her wrist absently as she watched him go. She turned to the other bartender and whispered something before disappearing into the back room.

"Alexi," Kate called, but Alexi was already gone. Kate rounded the bar and pushed through the door behind her. "Alexi, wait a minute." She finally caught up with her in a dimly lit storage room. Stacks of cardboard boxes bearing the logos of various liquors surrounded them.

"You're not supposed to be in here." Alexi spun around so quickly that, startled, Kate backed up.

"Are you okay?" Kate took Alexi's hand, intent on examining the reddened skin around her wrist, but Alexi pulled it back.

"I don't need you rescuing me."

"Really? Because it kind of looked like you did."

"I can take care of myself. And I could have resolved the situation without embarrassing him."

"Who the hell cares about him? Why should he get to save face in front of his buddies?"

"Because he's a customer, Kate."

"So he gets to treat you however he wants to?" Kate recaptured Alexi's hand and rubbed her thumb lightly over the inflamed skin. "He can do this?"

"No. But—" Alexi extricated her hand, more gently this time—"I know when to draw the line. And I would have asked one of the guys for help if I needed it."

"Would you have?"

"Yes."

"Then why is it so hard for you to accept my help?"

Alexi didn't answer, but she did look Kate in the eyes, and the conflict that Kate saw there gave her hope. She took a step closer.

"You can't let me in?"

Alexi laughed harshly. "No. That's far too scary."

"Look at me." Kate assumed her most innocent expression and took another step. "I'm not scary."

Alexi backed up a pace. "Oh, yes, you are."

"Really?" Kate was still within touching distance, but, fearful of pushing Alexi farther away, she kept her hands balled at her side.

Alexi nodded. "You might be the scariest person I've ever met."

"Why?" When Alexi remained silent, Kate wondered if she should back off. But despite Alexi's body language, something soft and needy remained in her eyes that compelled Kate to push. "Why are you afraid of me?"

"Because you make me want you," Alexi finally answered so quietly that Kate could barely hear her.

"I make you? And that's bad?"

"For me it is."

"Because you need to keep control. You can't give even an inch of it." Surprise flashed in Alexi's eyes. "You didn't think I understood that?"

Alexi shook her head and looked away.

"I'm not your enemy, Alexi." Kate touched Alexi's jaw.

Alexi jerked her chin away defiantly. "You thought I set my own bar on fire."

"I was doing my job. You do understand that I'm trying to help you, don't you?"

"When did you stop believing that I did it?"

Kate laced her fingers together and stared down at her hands. "I haven't wanted to believe it since the moment we met."

"But you did."

"Yes. At first, I thought it might be possible."

"And now?"

"Now, I know you're not about taking the easy way out. Even if you were in trouble, you would find another way."

"Just yesterday you thought this was a bad idea," Alexi said as she took Kate's hand.

"It probably still is." Kate drew Alexi closer and wrapped her arms around her. "But I don't really want to think about that right now."

Alexi stood within the circle of Kate's arms and wished they could disregard all the reasons why they shouldn't be involved. She couldn't remember the last time she was able to simply enjoy a woman's company without feeling as if she had to hide a part of herself. She entered each new relationship with fear and dread, already knowing how it would inevitably turn out and waiting the entire time for it to end.

When Alexi tilted her face upward, Kate was waiting. She covered her mouth in a slow, thorough kiss that drove all thoughts of the past from Alexi's mind. All that mattered was the taste of Kate's lips and the feel of Kate's hands stroking her back. Alexi rested her hands in the small of Kate's back, wrapped her fingers around the smooth leather of Kate's belt, and held on.

At the sound of a throat clearing behind her, Alexi pulled away quickly. Kate released her easily and she retreated into a wall of boxes. One of the waitresses stood in the doorway.

"I'm sorry to interrupt, but Frankie needs your help behind the bar," she said before she withdrew from the room and closed the door behind her.

"I better to get back to work." Part of Alexi was glad for the interruption because the rational part of her wondered how far she would have let things go. The flash of excitement along her spine at the thought of a quickie in the storeroom with Kate was out of character for Alexi. She'd never wanted so much to ignore the logical voice in her head.

CHAPTER SIXTEEN

Kate rolled over, grabbed her pager from the bedside table, and jabbed the button to stop the piercing beep that had ripped her from a sound sleep. It was just midnight, but Kate had already been deeply asleep for two hours. She and Jason had been on call since yesterday, and when the day had passed without a serious fire, Kate had been hopeful they wouldn't get a new case. She squinted at the display until the message came into focus, then forced herself out of bed.

A quick shower, just warm enough to be barely tolerable, woke her up, and she put on her uniform as if on autopilot. She pulled her hair into a neat bun and quickly applied her makeup. Just because it was the middle of the night was no reason not to be presentable.

She tucked her wallet in her pocket and searched for her keys, which she finally located in the pocket of her jacket hanging behind the door, then headed out to the Tahoe. On the way there, Jason called. One of his boys had a fever, and he wanted to know if she would mind taking this call on her own. She had just assured him that she would be fine and hung up the phone as she pulled up on scene.

After getting her gear from the back of the Tahoe, Kate wove through the maze of fire engines and other apparatus. She found the incident commander standing near the engine closest to the hot zone. He was shouting instructions for salvage and recovery into his radio, and while Kate waited for him to finish she surveyed the scene. In front of her stood a one-story wood-frame residential structure. Though the exterior of the building had sustained fire damage on one side, it was not severe enough to compromise the structural integrity. The flames had been extinguished and now firefighters checked for hot spots.

"Hey, Chief. What have you got?" Kate asked when he shoved his radio back in the front pocket of his turnout coat.

"The call came in from a neighbor. The residents reported that the fire started in the kitchen, an unattended pot on the stove."

"At this time of night?"

He shrugged. "They were still trying to put it out when the first unit arrived. But there was a lot of clutter in the kitchen and the fire spread fast."

"Where is the neighbor?"

"She went back inside her house to make coffee for the guys." He pointed at a house to the right.

"I'll take some photos first, then I need to talk to her as well as the residents."

"We'll make sure nobody goes anywhere."

As she circled the exterior of the house, Kate carefully reviewed her checklist in her head. Jason trusted her to handle the documentation of this scene and she wanted to be as thorough as possible. She found no evidence that the fire started outside so when she returned to the front of the house, she went inside.

The entryway wasn't damaged, but the smell of smoke still hung in the air. As she passed through the living room and into the kitchen she started seeing signs of fire. Kate began to photograph the room from several angles. Char patterns crept up the walls, where they weren't completely blackened. The range had been pulled to the center of the room by firefighters checking for fire behind it. Small remnants of a curtain, now black, clung to a rod over the window. The countertops were littered with unrecognizable rubble, burnt and soggy.

"I don't think these people threw anything away," one of firefighters said as Kate passed.

On the dinette table, Kate found the remains of what she guessed used to be a stack of newspapers and magazines. A warped pot sat on the stovetop, and whatever had been inside was indistinguishable now.

By the time she'd finished in the kitchen, Kate was fairly certain that this fire was accidental. The arson rate in Nashville was fairly low, and she was fast learning that their goal when investigating the majority of the fires was to rule out arson rather than prove it.

Outside she found the residents, a young couple who had moved into the house only a month ago. They both worked the second shift at a warehouse downtown and had been pulling in a ton of overtime. After work that night, they had begun to make dinner and had both fallen asleep on the sofa. They awoke to the smell of smoke and the smoke detectors going off, but instead of calling for help and vacating the house, they had tried to extinguish the blaze themselves.

"What do we do now? We used all of our savings to buy this place," the young woman asked as she clung to her husband. He wrapped his arm tight around her, but could not provide any answers.

"Do you have homeowners' insurance?" Kate asked.

"Honey?" The woman looked at her husband.

"Yes. We do."

"Contact them in the morning. They'll know how to obtain copies of our report. And they can tell you how to proceed."

"Okay."

"Is there someplace you can stay for a while?"

"We can stay with my mother," the woman said

The neighbor who called 9-1-1 didn't have much to add.

While taking her dog for his evening walk before bed, she saw the flames through the window. She ran back inside for her phone, then went next door to make sure her neighbors were awake.

By the time Kate took statements and contact information, the IC had terminated command and the firefighters had packed up the hose and left. Kate called the dispatcher to let him know she was clear from the call, then finished stowing her equipment in the Tahoe.

This had been one of those routine calls Jason talked about. No excitement here, but just as in the Hertz case, Kate had a role to fill. This time it might not be as dramatic as court testimony, but her report mattered to this young couple who would need their insurance money to rebuild their first home together.

It was nearly four a.m. when Kate finally pulled back into the parking lot of her apartment building. She had gone by the office and dropped off her notes and evidence from the fire, then, deciding the work would still be there in the morning, she returned home to get a couple more hours of sleep.

She got out of the Tahoe and grabbed the bag containing her camera from the back compartment. Though she lived in a fairly safe neighborhood, she didn't take any chances with the valuable equipment.

As she walked up the steps she saw someone turn away from her door. Her pulse quickened as she recognized the tall figure. Alexi shoved her hands into her jacket pockets and came back down the breezeway toward Kate.

"Hey," Kate said when she was close enough to be heard.

"Oh, hi. I thought you were inside. I didn't knock because I figured it was too late—or early."

"You came all the way over here to stand outside my door, then leave."

"When you put it that way it sounds silly. But, yes, I guess

I did. I closed at the bar and when I got in the car, it just kind of steered its way over here. But when I got here, I decided not to knock."

"Well, since you're here you can at least come in for a drink."

"No, thank you," Alexi replied with a harsh laugh.

"I meant—I have diet soda, water, or juice."

"That's okay."

"Are you sure? It's apple juice."

"I'm sure. But don't let that stop you from having what you want."

"What I want?"

Kate's voice was soft and intimate, and Alexi had no problem imagining what Kate might want. "To—um—drink." Alexi cleared her throat. "Don't feel like you can't have a drink, just because I'm an—have whatever you'd like."

"Why don't you just come in and we'll figure it out."

Kate hitched her bag higher on her shoulder and flipped her keys in her hand until she had the right one. Alexi couldn't explain why she was here or even what she expected to happen. But she hadn't stopping thinking about that kiss all night, often stopping in the middle of filling an order to touch her fingers to her lips as if she could still feel it. So when she left work, she'd ended up here, standing outside Kate's door and wishing she could set aside the events of the past week and a half. She wanted to act without thinking, and she couldn't recall the last time she'd done that without alcohol as an excuse for ignoring her inhibitions.

She followed Kate inside and remembered the last time she'd been here when she'd awakened in Kate's bed. She had been embarrassed and illogically resentful toward Kate for seeing her at her most vulnerable. If someone had told her then that she would be here now, she would have thought they were crazy.

Kate dropped her bag inside the foyer and her keys on the table nearby. She shrugged out of her jacket and hung it on a hook behind the door.

"Can I take your coat?" She slipped it off Alexi's shoulders and hung it next to her own.

Alexi turned to face her and noticed the smudges on Kate's cheek and forehead that she hadn't seen in the darkened breezeway. The sharp odor of smoke stung her nose.

"Were you working?"

"Yes, I got called in." Kate sniffed and stepped backward. "I need to take a shower. Why don't you make yourself comfortable in the living room and I'll be right back."

"Maybe I should go. This wasn't a good idea."

Kate smiled. "Yeah. We keep saying that. Please don't go anywhere. I'll only be a few minutes."

Kate disappeared down the hallway toward the bedroom before Alexi could argue. She heard the shower come on before Kate closed the door. Alexi wandered into the living room, but instead of settling on the sofa, she circled the room. A fireplace was centered on one wall and above it hung a flat-screen television.

But Alexi was more interested in the framed photos placed along the mantle. She'd found she could get a real sense of someone by the photographs they displayed. Alexi's own walls were decorated with pictures of her and her father. In the occasional shot with her mother, both Alexi and her mother stood stiffly, as if they were enduring the picture rather than enjoying it.

Kate had five matching black frames, and most of the contents had a similar theme as well. Kate and three men posed in front of a fire engine, and Alexi guessed she was looking at Kate's old crew. In another shot, Kate stood between two men. All three wore T-shirts bearing fire-department logos. Though neither of the men looked like Kate, they looked enough alike for Alexi to be sure they were related, and she thought she detected a similarity in the wide grins on all three faces. Kate's brother and father, most likely. Another photo was taken in a kitchen. Kate stood behind a much shorter woman with both arms wrapped around her. Here was the source of Kate's features. Matching sets of green eyes looked back at the camera. Alexi could easily imagine that Kate would look just like her mother in twenty years or so. There was a photo of Kate and a woman Alexi had seen at the bar with her. And the last one was of two small boys climbing on a fire engine while Kate's brother looked on.

"My nephews," Kate said as she came from the bedroom.

"They're cute." Alexi turned and drew a quick breath. The shapeless gray sweats weren't attractive in the least. But Kate's face, freshly scrubbed and free of makeup, was beautiful. Her hair was still wet and she had left it loose.

"Yeah, when they're sleeping. Otherwise, they are little balls of energy." Kate rounded the sofa and sat down. She moved with a natural confidence that made her attractive even in the most casual setting. "You can come over here. I promise I smell better now."

Alexi sat next her and immediately felt awkward. "I'm sorry. I shouldn't be here. It's late and you probably have to get up for work in a few hours."

"Yes, I do." Kate touched the back of Alexi's hand, and Alexi turned hers over and slipped her fingers between Kate's. "But right now I'm not very tired. Finding you on my doorstep was a pleasant surprise."

Alexi moved closer and, with her free hand, tucked a strand of hair behind Kate's ear. "Can we not discuss it?"

"Discuss what?" Kate stroked Alexi's cheek.

"What we both know we're about to do."

"Are you going to regret it in the morning?"

"It *is* morning." Alexi traced the neck of Kate's sweatshirt and dipped her fingers inside.

"Answer the question."

"Maybe," Alexi answered honestly. "But isn't it enough that I want it now?"

"Alexi—"

"I haven't done anything without analyzing it to death in so long."

"I'm not interested in being part of some experiment—"

"I know that." Alexi rubbed one finger across Kate's lower lip. "That's not what I meant. I know that if this is more than a one-night thing we have a lot of issues to work out. I'm only asking for right now that we don't have to be those two people." She kissed Kate's neck.

"Well, how can I resist when you're doing that?"

"Hmm, that's just it. I don't want you to resist." Alexi left a trail of kisses over her jaw and cheek.

Kate guided Alexi's mouth to hers and when they met, what began as gentle persuasion flared into a heated exchange. Kate couldn't have dampened the inferno that engulfed them and she didn't want to. Alexi's lips moved against hers aggressively, then when Alexi tore her mouth away, they traced a hot path down the side of her neck.

Alexi shoved her hands into Kate's hair and tugged her head to the side. When Kate reached for the hem of Alexi's shirt, Alexi batted her hands away. She pulled Kate into her lap and Kate shifted so she could straddle Alexi's lap, squeezing her knees against the outside of Alexi's hips.

Alexi lifted Kate's sweatshirt and touched the bare skin of Kate's stomach. She stroked her hands upward and brushed the underside of Kate's breasts. Kate pulled her sweatshirt off and tossed it aside.

"Every time I saw you, I wanted to find out what was under your uniform," Alexi whispered, tilting her head back to meet Kate's eyes. "So proper and perfectly pressed."

Kate frowned down at her chest. She cupped her own breasts in her hands and lifted them slightly. They weren't as perky as they'd been in her twenties. "Not so perfect underneath," she murmured.

Alexi leaned forward and kissed Kate's nipple. "Just right," she said against Kate's skin, then pulled back and traced her finger in a circle on Kate's other breast.

Kate closed her eyes as Alexi teased the edge of her areola, and tiny points of pleasure flashed through her and settled low in her belly. Alexi maintained the gentle pressure even when Kate couldn't help arching into her touch. Alexi's breath feathered against Kate's sensitive skin and she imagined she could feel the warm, wet sensation of Alexi's mouth.

Kate wrapped one hand around the back of Alexi's neck and urged her closer. Alexi complied, first teasing Kate with a swipe of her tongue, then covering her nipple and sucking it. Kate rested her other palm against the back of Alexi's head and held her close while Alexi played her tongue and teeth over Kate's nipple. Alexi's arms came around Kate and she swept her fingers inside the waistband of Kate's pants.

Need swelled within Kate, nearly overwhelming her desire to let Alexi set the pace. When all she could think about was pushing Alexi back on the sofa and touching every inch of her, Kate decided it was time to slow the pace. She slid off Alexi's lap and took her hand. As she walked into her bedroom, Alexi was right behind her, pushing her sweatpants over her hips. Kate stepped out of them and continued to the bed. She turned and laid her hands on Alexi's chest, her fingers resting on the ridges of Alexi's collarbones. But when she opened the top button of Alexi's shirt, Alexi gripped her wrists and stilled her hands.

"I'm already so far ahead. You've got some catching up to do," Kate said. She glanced down. She was wearing only her panties and Alexi was still fully dressed.

"Later."

"I want to feel you against me."

Alexi unbuttoned her shirt and slipped it off her shoulders, but instead of taking off her bra she urged Kate onto the bed and moved over her. Alexi pressed her hands on the bed above Kate's shoulders, holding her weight while she kissed Kate again. The position forced her hips firmly against Kate's, and Kate took advantage of their closeness by thrusting her hips upward. The sweet ache that had been building between her legs intensified with the pressure and Kate couldn't contain a low moan.

Alexi's answering growl vibrated in her chest and she lifted her hips away. She covered Kate's breast, gently pinching her nipple.

"Harder," Kate urged. Pain-laced pleasure shot through her and drew another moan from her throat. She dropped her head back, and Alexi took the opportunity to close her teeth on her neck.

Kate wrapped her arms around Alexi's back and pulled her down. She might have expected the feeling of security at having Alexi's weight settle over her. But the thrill of powerlessness was a pleasant surprise. Alexi swept her hand over Kate's stomach and the sensitive skin there danced in response. When she covered Kate's center, over the triangle of cotton, Kate's hips bucked.

"That's not enough." Kate caught Alexi's hand and pushed it inside her panties. Alexi rose to her knees, then bent forward to press her mouth to Kate's stomach.

"Lift," she whispered against Kate's navel. She eased Kate's panties down her legs and off.

She pressed her hand against Kate's center. The feel of Alexi's mouth on her skin and the sensation of warm fingers on her already heated flesh melded into a molten throb that began deep inside and pulsated outward to her clitoris.

Through the fog that threatened to steal her ability to form a conscious thought, Kate reached for Alexi's waistband, intent on opening her fly. She closed her hand around the denim, but then Alexi slipped her fingers down and inside, pressing deep. Kate's fingers lost their purpose, and the button on Alexi's fly became an anchor—the only thing keeping Kate from drifting away completely.

"I want to touch you," Kate managed.

"I want—" Alexi moved over Kate—"this." She began with a long slow thrust that escalated to match the pace of Kate's hips rising in response.

She carried Kate so close to the edge that Kate thought she might splinter into pieces, then she backed off and stroked alongside her clitoris frustratingly slowly. When Kate writhed and whimpered beneath her, Alexi slipped back inside to begin the climb again.

"Please, let me—now," Kate finally begged after Alexi eased up once more. She framed Alexi's face and when she slid her hands to Alexi's neck, Alexi's pulse jumped wildly against her palms.

This time, Kate lifted her knee until her thigh rode between Alexi's legs with the motion of Alexi's thrusts. Alexi's eyes were dark and full of need and desire, and she kept them locked on Kate's face. She pulled her lower lip between her teeth and surged inside Kate, hard and fast, her hips rocking in unison. Kate held Alexi's gaze as long as she could, but when the searing pleasure of Alexi's fingers and the feel of Alexi grinding against her leg became too much, she slammed her eyes closed and surrendered. She dug her fingers into the back of Alexi's neck as her body convulsed.

Alexi pressed her forehead to Kate's, and from somewhere else Kate registered the erratic twitch of Alexi's hips just before Alexi rolled to her side and pulled Kate close.

CHAPTER SEVENTEEN

Alexi awoke wrapped in white linens that smelled like flowers. But this time instead of confusion about how she ended up there, she felt only satisfaction. She pushed back the covers and smiled when she saw the same blue T-shirt with the fire-department logo. Kate had coaxed her into it just before they both fell asleep. She glanced at the clock on the bedside table and groaned when she realized that had been a little more than an hour ago. At least she didn't have to work until that afternoon. She could go home and grab a few more hours sleep before then.

Kate was the one who had to work early this morning. Alexi was actually impressed to hear the shower running already. She rolled to her side and looked at the empty span of bed next to her. The pillow still held an indentation from Kate's head, and when Alexi slid her hand across the sheet, it was still warm.

She felt surprisingly okay about what had happened between them, despite the fact that it had been the first time she'd been with anyone since she got sober. She might be ready, she realized for the first time. She might be ready, and that thought didn't scare her nearly as much as it should have. Sure, she was a work in progress, but who wasn't. A year ago she'd vowed to make a change in her life—a change that centered around making herself a better person. That plan hadn't left room for a relationship.

And though she wasn't done changing yet, she'd actually come a long way from the mess she had been a year ago, even when she considered her latest lapse.

Did she want to be involved with Kate? When she'd shown up outside Kate's door this morning, she had half expected Kate to turn her away—had actually been more prepared for that than for what had happened. But now, she realized, she could be ready for a real relationship. While she would forever be an alcoholic, she could minimize the effect that fact had on her life. She could have a healthy relationship. That was perhaps her biggest revelation. And whether things worked out with Kate or not, the knowledge that she was capable of such a connection lifted a weight from Alexi's shoulders.

When she'd been drinking, she had gravitated toward women who didn't ask too many questions and who would accept her bullshit answers when they did. Self-involved women didn't notice when Alexi's lies fell apart or when she held them at arm's length. If she paid them enough attention, they didn't pick up on the times when mentally she wasn't really there.

Alexi's first impression, which she admitted was based on appearance alone, was that Kate Chambers might be one of those women. But, she now knew, Kate didn't even come close to falling into that category. Kate paid attention to those around her, probably picking up on more than anyone realized. Alexi wouldn't be able to hide as much of herself from Kate as she did from everyone else in her life. Something told her Kate wouldn't be content with Alexi's half-hearted assurances. *Am I ready for that?*

From the bathroom she heard singing and she smiled. Perhaps she'd just discovered the one thing Kate wasn't good at. Despite the lauded shower acoustics, Kate was extremely off-key.

Alexi slipped out of bed and padded into the bathroom. A warm mist of steam filled the room. She grabbed a towel from the bar inside the door just as the shower turned off.

"You have a lovely voice," she teased, opening the towel in front of her. "Why didn't you wake me?"

"I figured I'd let you sleep while I got ready for work." Kate stepped close and kissed her.

Alexi wrapped the towel around Kate and held her captive for a moment. "Did you get any sleep?"

"Enough."

"You'll be exhausted today."

Kate shrugged inside the towel. "I'll live. It was worth it." She grinned.

"Better hurry or you'll be late." Alexi released her and returned to the bedroom. She decided to forego her own shower until she got home. Reluctantly, she took off Kate's shirt and put on her own. She found her jeans in a heap on the floor and was just stepping into them when Kate braced her shoulder on the doorjamb between the bathroom and bedroom. Her towel encircled her torso and was secured just above her breasts, leaving her smooth, pale legs bare. Alexi felt a flush creep up her neck and a renewed rush of arousal when she recalled the sensation of them wrapped around her.

"Are you leaving?"

"Yes." Alexi checked her pockets for her wallet and cell phone.

"You're going to sleep when you get home, aren't you?"

Alexi grinned guiltily. "Yeah. Would it make you feel better if I promise to dream about you?"

Kate tilted her head to the side. "Maybe. Because I will probably be sitting at my desk thinking about you in bed."

"I guess that's better than you falling asleep at your desk." Alexi headed for the bedroom door, and Kate followed her through it and down the hallway. She grabbed her jacket from behind the door and fished her keys out of the pocket.

"Hey," Kate said when Alexi had her hand on the doorknob. Releasing it, she turned around. "Are you okay about this?"

Touched by the sincerity in Kate's voice, Alexi answered honestly. "For now."

"No morning regrets?"

"None."

"And otherwise? I'm sorry. I haven't even bothered to ask how everything else is."

"Well, on top of all my other stress, Danielle and I aren't really getting along."

"Why not?"

"I'm not sure. We argued the other day and we're both too stubborn to apologize, I guess. I feel like she's choosing Ron over me." Alexi shrugged. "That sounds kind of selfish when I say it out loud. I'm sure she'll come around eventually. I'd better let you get ready for work."

"Can I call you later?"

"I'd like that."

"Okay." Kate grasped the edges of Alexi's jacket and pulled her close for one more kiss, this time lingering to caress Alexi's lips slowly. When Alexi felt Kate's tongue slide against hers, she tugged the corner of Kate's towel free. But Kate caught it against her before it could drop. She released Alexi and playfully pushed her away. "Okay. You go now."

"Spoilsport."

"You're dragging in late this morning," Jason said as he stood and crossed to get some pages off the printer.

Kate glanced at her watch. "I'm not late."

"You're not as early as you usually are."

"I stopped for coffee. The good stuff." She smiled and lifted the cardboard drink carrier in her hand. "I brought you one, too."

Jason watched her a little too closely as she set a cup on his desk and one on her own.

"Anyone I know?"

"What?"

"I haven't seen you grin like that since you started working over here. Since I doubt it's the job, it must be a man. So is he a firefighter? Someone I know?"

Normally, Kate would blow off any questions about her personal life or make a joke to change the subject. But she liked Jason, and she didn't get the impression that he would be judgmental or treat her differently.

"It's not a man, Jason."

"Well, what else could it be? I know you're not suddenly giddy over the job. Was that fire last night really all that exciting?"

"It's not a *man*."

Jason was silent for a minute and Kate could almost see his brain working. The wave of disbelief on his face when he figured it out would actually have been comical if Kate wasn't nervous about his response.

"No way. You're way too pretty to be a—" He stopped quickly, censoring himself a little too late.

Kate laughed. "Oh, I really want to know what word you were going to use just then."

"I—well, you're gorgeous. You could have any guy you want."

"Jason, women aren't lesbians because they can't get a man."

"I know, I know. But you—okay, I need a minute to take this in." He sat down and sipped his coffee. He looked at her, then away, then back at her again.

"Should I not have told you?" Kate picked up her notes from the previous night's fire and started up her computer.

"No, no. It doesn't change what I think about you." He flipped through his reports, signing in the appropriate places. After a minute of silence, he said, "If there's no man, then who's the woman?"

Kate hesitated.

"What? You're not going to tell me. You drop this on me and you won't even give me the details?"

"I'm not sure you'll approve."

"Why wouldn't I—"

"It's Alexi Clark," Kate blurted before she could change her mind. Just saying Alexi's name brought visions of the previous night into her head. Alexi had been amazing and attentive. And Kate's only complaint was that whenever she'd tried to return the favor, Alexi had turned things around and made love to Kate once more. And though it hardly seemed that was something worth complaining about, instead of feeling completely sated, Kate wanted Alexi more than ever. Today, in addition to having the feel of Alexi's hands and mouth imprinted on her skin, Kate was still imagining how Alexi's body would feel beneath her hands, and she thought she might go mad before the end of the day.

Jason sat quietly for so long that Kate got nervous. "Please, say something. I didn't mean for it to happen."

"You should be careful, Kate."

"I know it doesn't seem like the best idea." Being with Alexi was the one thing Kate hadn't had to analyze to death in months. When she was with Alexi, she no longer felt like she was half of what she used to be—she no longer felt like she would forever be incomplete without firefighting in her life. Alexi made her believe she could be whole, like she could be happy in her new circumstances.

"Doesn't seem like it? It's not a good idea at all."

"If I thought for a second she could be the one who set those fires, I wouldn't have let anything happen."

"I would hope not. What happened? Was this some kind of booty call or something?"

"No," Kate exclaimed. She and Alexi hadn't talked much about what it had meant; Alexi had insisted on that at first. Then this morning, Kate hadn't wanted to ruin the lingering intimacy between them. Was this a fling for Alexi? She didn't think so. Alexi had suggested that if they were talking about more than just one night they would need to address some issues. That didn't sound like Alexi was intent on a one-night stand. And this morning, she hadn't seemed in a hurry to leave like one might expect if she didn't want them to continue seeing each other. In fact, they had even taken time for a little small talk about Alexi's problems with Danielle.

Suddenly, Kate replayed Alexi's words. *I feel like she's choosing Ron over me.* She pushed aside her notes from last night's fire and searched for her file on Alexi's fire. She flipped rapidly through pages of reports.

"What are you looking for?" Jason asked.

"Something I missed." Kate scanned the page in front of her. "Alexi said that she and Ron were the only ones with keys to the garage, but that most of the contents were Alexi's personal property. She said Ron never went in there."

"So?"

"So, what about Danielle Volk?"

"I don't remember any mention of whether she goes in there or not."

"We found her prints on the gas can, on the workbench near where the can was stored, and on the padlock."

"Weren't she and Alexi Clark best friends?"

"Yeah, I know. And that's why I didn't think anything of it, initially. Maybe I'm way off base here." Kate shook her head, trying to keep her thoughts in line. "But Alexi said something that made me wonder if Danielle was as loyal to Alexi as we assumed."

"Pillow talk?"

"Shut up, I'm serious. Danielle comes off as supportive and a little meek. But a couple of times I've wondered if we underestimated her. Maybe if she thought she was protecting her husband, she's capable of more than anyone gives her credit for."

"Let's ask her. See if she can come in this afternoon."

"I need to make a phone call first." Kate ignored Jason's

look of disapproval and flipped open her cell phone. "If we're about to shatter their friendship, I owe Alexi that much."

❖

"Right through here," Kate said as she led Danielle Volk into the conference room. "Mr. Hayworth will be right with us. Have a seat." Kate closed the door behind them.

As Danielle pulled out a chair on the opposite side of the table, she gave Kate a curious look, but Kate wasn't ready to divulge anything just yet.

"You don't mind if we record this interview, do you?" Kate fiddled with the small video camera she'd set up on the table earlier.

"I guess not."

"Good." Kate engaged the camera as Jason entered the room. He crossed to stand against the wall on Danielle's left. When Kate glanced at Jason, he nodded for her to begin the questioning.

"Mrs. Volk, is there anything else you want to tell us about the night of the fire at In Left Field?"

"No." Danielle held Kate's gaze, unblinking. Kate hadn't expected such a general, open-ended question to trip Danielle up, but she wanted a baseline to gauge Danielle's reactions.

"Can you explain why we found your prints on the gas can in Alexi's garage?"

"I must have borrowed it."

"Did you also borrow your husband's keys to the garage behind the bar?"

"Not that I can recall." Kate almost admired her steady nerves. If Danielle was experiencing any stress about the direction of Kate's questions, she wasn't showing any outward evidence of it.

"Yours and Alexi's were the only prints on the padlock."

"Well, maybe I did and I just don't remember."

"I have a theory about what might have happened that night. Would you like to hear it?"

"Not particularly." Venom crept into Danielle's voice but her expression remained placid.

"I think you knew about your husband's gambling problem and were looking for a way to help him out." Kate pulled out the chair across from Danielle and sat down.

"My husband's personal finances don't have anything to do with the bar."

"They do when he was taking money from the business account." Kate saw a slight tightening around Danielle's mouth. Apparently Alexi hadn't told Danielle that she'd disclosed this information to Kate.

"How much longer do you think Ms. Clark would have put up with him stealing from the bar?" Jason asked.

When Danielle didn't answer, Kate said, "I got the impression she was about fed up. She'd finally gotten her life straightened out, but now she had to deal with Ron's problems."

"What has she been telling you?" Danielle snapped, and Kate glimpsed the first crack in her façade. Kate had purposely implied that she'd had detailed and perhaps personal conversations with Alexi about her feelings regarding Ron's gambling, and the flash of jealousy in Danielle's eyes didn't disappoint her.

Kate ignored the question. "An insurance payout would have solved his financial problems as well as given him the opportunity to convince Alexi to dissolve their partnership."

Danielle glared at Kate.

Kate chuckled and looked at Jason. "I wish I could have heard that conversation, don't you?" She shifted her gaze back to Danielle. "After everything you've been through together, can you imagine how it must have made her feel to know that you both wanted to abandon her?" Kate was speculating now, but Danielle's hardening expression told her she was hitting the mark.

"Everything we've been through?" Danielle no longer made any attempt to hide the bitterness in her voice. "Most of it was her fault. We put up with her drinking for far too many years."

"That's right. You took care of her when she couldn't even get through a day without a drink. I can't even imagine how many times she must have hurt you, yet you kept coming back for more."

"No one would have blamed us if we had given up on her a long time ago. Even her own mother hasn't spoken to her in years."

Momentarily stunned, Kate could only stare at Danielle. She could imagine the damage that statement, so coldly spoken, would inflict. And she suddenly regretted her role in this conversation. But she hadn't come this far to back down. She needed the truth so she forced out the words that would spur Danielle's resentment.

"So where is her sympathy when your husband has his own addiction?"

"Ron does *not* have an addiction. He made a few bad bets."

Kate stood. "Denial, huh? Perhaps you both have a problem. Maybe you should reconsider, because it sounds like you all have the perfect partnership—one big dysfunctional family."

"You don't know anything about my life." Danielle slammed her hands on the table and leapt to her feet.

"Sit down, Mrs. Volk."

"You don't understand the sacrifices I've made for that damn bar. The time that place has consumed from our lives. And what do we have to show for it now. Nothing."

"And whose fault is that?"

Danielle didn't hesitate. "Alexi's. It's her fault. She wanted that place so bad and she dragged my husband into it."

"That's not how I heard it. He was more than happy to invest in the place. After all, he knew a good thing when he saw it. She would work her ass off to make it great, and he could hitch a ride on her success." Kate was on a roll now, and she couldn't stop her responses anymore than Danielle probably could have. Kate glanced at Jason and saw surprise on his face, but no sign that he wanted her to stop.

"Bullshit. Alexi needed him. She never would have survived those first few years without us."

"She's never been sufficiently grateful, has she?"

"Grateful? When my friends my age were having kids and taking family vacations, I was stuck in that bar or at home alone because Ron kept such long hours there."

"You've been sacrificing for years. So when Ron got in trouble, it was someone else's turn. Even if that meant Alexi losing her bar." Kate wanted to point out that Ron found time for gambling, but she didn't because she needed to keep Danielle's attention focused on Alexi as the catalyst for her problems.

"Damn right. I did what I had to do. For my family."

"That sounded like an admission of guilt," Jason said quietly in the silence that followed Danielle's outburst.

Kate heard the click of the conference room door opening behind her and closed her eyes briefly. Without even turning around she could feel the hurt radiating from Alexi, and she felt partially responsible. She'd goaded Danielle to the point of frustration and had actually felt relieved when she cracked.

"What exactly did you do?" Alexi's voice was laced with pain and disbelief. She moved to stand opposite Danielle, and now Kate could see the hollowness in her eyes.

"What are you doing here?" Obviously shocked, Danielle backed up a step and nearly tripped over the chair she'd shoved back.

Jason pushed off the wall and pointed at the video camera on the table. "That's a Wi-Fi camera. She's been watching in the next room."

Danielle looked at him in disbelief, then turned to Alexi, her expression beseeching. "Ron was in so deep and he wouldn't stop making bets. He thought he could somehow make things better with just one big win. I just couldn't see any other way out."

Alexi stared at her. Kate wanted to take her hand and let

her know she wasn't alone. But aside from the gesture being unprofessional, Kate wasn't sure it would be welcome.

"It wasn't supposed to be this complicated. After the fire at the bar, I thought the insurance company would just pay up and we'd all move on." Danielle was still trying to convince Alexi that she had done the right thing, as if she could somehow justify what she'd said only moments ago.

"How could you do this?"

"I didn't know what else to do."

"So, the garage, was that you too?" Alexi's eyes filled with tears and her jaw tightened as if she were trying to keep them from falling.

Until that moment Danielle had been able to look at Alexi, but now her gaze dropped to the table in front of her.

"Answer me," Alexi demanded.

Danielle flinched. "I wanted to scare you. When you told me you'd been to see Anthony Wilde, I panicked. All your questions were causing problems and you wouldn't let it go. I was afraid of exactly this scenario."

"It's my fault?" Alexi's voice shook. "You're actually telling me it's my fault you set that fire in my garage." Alexi folded her arms over her stomach and Kate thought she might double over.

"Alexi—"

"You knew. You knew how much that bar meant to me. There was another way, we could have figured out another…and my father's car…" Alexi's voice cracked.

Kate's heart broke for her even while she was furious at Danielle for making Alexi feel she was responsible.

"Alexi, we've been friends for a long time. When you've calmed down, you'll see that I did what was best."

"What you did—was unforgivable." Alexi turned and walked out without waiting for a response.

Danielle looked at the camera on the table, then at Kate and Jason. "What happens now?" she asked with resignation.

Jason answered. "I suggest you speak to an attorney. You'll be hearing from someone in the DA's office."

By the time Kate was able to escape from the conference room, Alexi was long gone. She debated trying to call her, but was uncertain how she would respond. She wanted to go to her, but everything she knew about Alexi told her that she probably needed some space to process what had just happened.

CHAPTER EIGHTEEN

"I'm sorry. I don't know what I'm doing here," Alexi said as soon as Kate opened her apartment door.

Kate stepped back. "Come in."

Alexi remained standing on the threshold. "Normally, I go to Danielle when I need to talk, but…"

Alexi looked exhausted, her eyes were red, as if she'd been crying, and the skin under them appeared bruised. Kate suspected that only sheer will held her upright.

"I'm glad you're here." Kate took Alexi's hand and guided her inside. Alexi didn't even seem to notice when Kate led her to the couch and settled her there. "I'm sorry about what happened today."

"Why? You were only doing your job." A trace of bitterness permeated Alexi's voice.

"That's not why I'm sorry. I know how much this hurt you."

A muscle jumped in Alexi's jaw as she clenched her teeth. "I'll be okay."

Kate still held Alexi's hand and she rubbed her thumb against the base of Alexi's. "So you came here just to continue shutting me out."

"I told you, I don't know why I'm here."

"You said you needed to talk. So, please, talk to me." Kate's cell phone rang and she glanced at the display. "Damn, I have to get this. I'll be right back." She flipped open her phone as she headed down the hallway. "Hey, Jason, what's up?"

"I'm sorry to bother you at home but the assistant district attorney called. She has to move our meeting from tomorrow afternoon to first thing in the morning. I have to drop the boys off at school, so I'll just meet you over there. Can you run by the office and grab the case file and the video from Danielle Volk's interview yesterday. They'll want copies of all that."

"Sure. No problem."

"Great. I'll see you tomorrow."

"Bright and early."

Jason laughed. "Yeah. Don't stay up too late."

"I'll try not to."

Kate closed her phone and returned to the living room but found it empty.

"Alexi," she called as she stuck her head into the kitchen. Alexi wasn't in there so she headed for the dining room.

In the doorway, Kate jerked to a stop, then forced herself to take several slow steps into the room. Alexi sat at the table, staring at a half-full bottle of Jack Daniels. Tears trickled down her cheeks and she seemed oblivious to Kate's presence.

"I, uh…" She didn't know what to say. But the apology she'd nearly made for having liquor in her own house would have sounded ridiculous. Alexi spent most of her time surrounded by bottles. She poured drinks all day long, so one bottle in Kate's cabinet wasn't that big a deal.

"The funny thing is—I don't even like whiskey." Alexi sniffed and swiped the back of her hand under her nose. Kate didn't drink whiskey either. The bottle was left over from a birthday party she'd thrown for Paula months ago. Realizing she should at least take the bottle out of the room, Kate stepped forward and reached for it, but Alexi's sharp words stopped her. "Leave it."

"Alexi—"

"I'm just looking at it."

"You don't need to."

"Yes. I do." When Alexi glanced at her, Kate felt a twinge in her chest at the pain pooling in her eyes. And as she watched, Alexi pulled the shutters down over those emotions. But, though they were now hidden, Kate sensed they were still there.

"Why? When I can take it away?"

"I don't need you to."

"I want to." She refused to let Alexi shut her out completely.

"I know you want to help, Kate. But you can't fix this."

Kate pulled out the chair next to Alexi's and sat. She reached for Alexi's hand, but Alexi pulled it free and tucked it in her lap. "I can if you'll let me."

"I can't let you. You're not always going to be there to eliminate the temptation."

"I'm here now. Why isn't that enough?"

Alexi wrapped her arms around her own torso, effectively forming a barrier between them. "It just isn't."

"Can I call someone for you? Your sponsor?" Kate braced herself for the answer, trying to convince herself not to take it personally if Alexi needed him instead of her.

"No."

"Alexi, it's okay to need someone, to ask for help. Isn't that something they teach in those programs?"

"Not this time. I have to be strong enough to do this on my own."

"Why is that so important now?"

"I need to trust myself, if I ever expect anyone else to trust me. And I want—" Alexi bit off her words.

"What?"

"Never mind." Alexi shook her head.

"Please." Kate touched Alexi's shoulder. "What do you want?"

"I want you to trust me." Alexi gazed at her with eyes that

were soft and unexpectedly open. A seed of hope unfurled in Kate's heart. Even if Alexi couldn't admit it yet, a part of her wanted to remove the wall between them. They just might have to do it one brick at a time.

"If this is what you need, then I'll let you have it." Kate squeezed Alexi's shoulder, then stood. "But I'm not going anywhere. I'll be in the next room when you're done."

Kate wanted more than anything to take that bottle away. But if Alexi needed to prove something, Kate would support her. She forced herself out of the room and into the bedroom, half hoping Alexi would call out to her. But she didn't. So Kate sat on her bed and picked up a book from the nightstand.

Alexi wasn't sure if Kate truly understood why she hadn't let her take the whiskey. But she'd given Alexi space anyway. Alexi stared at the bottle in front of her. She'd felt this pull before, the promise of a magical elixir to eradicate her pain. But, she now knew that was a lie. There was no magic and the pain did not go away; it only disappeared temporarily. The darkness turned inward and ate at her insides.

She needed to come to grips with what Danielle had done, and she would do so without alcohol. So she stayed rooted to her chair and stared at that bottle until her vision became hazy and her head ached. She and Danielle had been friends for almost half their lives. In all that time, she thought she knew Danielle as well as she knew herself. But she never would have believed Danielle capable of setting in motion the events that destroyed Alexi's whole life.

She'd put Danielle through hell over the years, and once she would have believed that meant she deserved what was happening to her now. But she'd since forgiven herself and asked Danielle and Ron to do the same. She thought they had. But for Danielle to forsake Alexi's dreams in order to protect Ron, she had to have been harboring at least a little resentment. Because the Danielle Alexi thought she knew could not have set that fire.

But she had. Not only that, but she'd admitted it to Alexi's face without a trace of remorse. Nothing Alexi could do would erase that betrayal. The only thing left for her to control was her own reaction to it.

❖

Kate heard the click of the bedroom door opening and looked up. Her book lay open on her lap but she hadn't turned a page in ten minutes. Alexi stood silhouetted in the doorway. Kate fought the urge to go to her. Instead she simply closed her book, set it aside, and waited. Alexi's eyes were shadowed and nothing in her posture gave a hint as to her state of mind.

"I didn't drink it," Alexi said softly.

"I didn't think you would."

Alexi crossed the room and crawled onto the bed next to Kate. "What if I had?"

Kate lifted her arm and Alexi moved under it and pressed closer. "Did you want to?"

"Yes. Well, sort of." Alexi laid her head on Kate's shoulder.

"I told you I wasn't going anywhere and I'm not." Kate kissed Alexi's forehead.

"You don't really know what I was like—what I can be like. I was angry and selfish and never concerned about anyone else as long as I got what I wanted. I've driven away plenty of people who vowed they wouldn't leave."

"And that's why you don't believe me when I say I won't."

"I want to."

"We have time. You're here now."

"I needed room to come to terms with things myself before I could share them with anyone."

Kate could understand that. She couldn't imagine finding out that the one person who knew her best in the world could destroy the thing that mattered most to her. And that's precisely why Kate had let her walk away that afternoon, but she'd also hoped Alexi would come to her when she was ready. And even though Alexi seemed reluctant to open up completely, Kate knew what a step forward it was that Alexi was lying next to her now.

"What stopped you from drinking tonight?"

"I don't want to be that person again. And I've accepted that I will never be someone who can drink casually. Besides, it's hard to not feel guilty now because I know what sobriety is like."

"And how is that?"

"I can feel when I'm sober. I used to drink to get numb." Alexi rested her hand on the center of Kate's chest and began to rub slow circles over Kate's T-shirt. "Finding out what Danielle did hurts like hell. But this—being with you feels good. And if I want that, I have to also take the pain in life."

"Alexi, before you decide if you want to be here with me, there's something you should know."

Alexi raised herself up on one elbow and moved her other hand down to Kate's stomach.

"We have to turn in our report to the insurance company."

"I know. I called them this afternoon and checked my policy. In the event of arson, our coverage allows for an innocent partner to collect. Assuming they believe I didn't have any knowledge of Danielle's actions, of course."

"So, what are you going to do?"

"What I had always planned. Rebuild and reopen." Alexi slipped her hand under the hem of Kate's T-shirt and traced tiny circles on her skin.

"That sounds like a good idea."

"Only this time, I'll be doing it by myself."

"No more partners?"

"No. This is my dream. I think I'm ready to tackle this one on my own now."

"Really?" Kate caught Alexi's hand in order to halt the stirring within her that those circles were causing. "Since you'll have the business under control, is there anything I can help you with?"

"I might be able to think of some way you can assist me." Alexi gently freed her hand and resumed the hypnotic caress. "Perhaps by helping me unwind after a stressful day of rebuilding my business—the occasional foot rub, maybe."

"Sure. And I could feed you grapes while you recline on the sofa."

"That sounds nice." Alexi's fingers wandered upward and toyed unhurriedly with Kate's nipple.

"Maybe we could start now." Kate rose and, with a hand on Alexi's shoulder, urged her to lie down.

"What do you mean?"

"Let me show you a little attention. Help you unwind." Kate touched Alexi's neck, tracing the tendons along the side of it.

"I'm not feeling all that stressed right now."

"Well, then let me wind you up first." Kate stroked down Alexi's arm and over her hip.

"Kate." Alexi rested her hand over Kate's, holding it in place.

"How long did you hope to keep distracting me?" Kate asked, momentarily allowing Alexi to stop her progress.

Alexi met Kate's eyes, imploring her to play along, but Kate purposely showed no indication that she would.

"You don't want me to touch you." Even as she said the words, Kate thought her heart might break if Alexi didn't deny it.

"It's not that—exactly."

"I know how much you need to be in control. But I need just as much for you to let go. Put yourself in my hands."

"I'm not sure I can."

"I promise I don't want you to do anything you don't want to. But will you hear me out first?"

"Okay."

Kate pressed her mouth close to Alexi's ear and whispered,

"Do you remember what it felt like last night when you were inside me?"

Alexi shivered against her. "Yes."

"Did it make you feel strong? Powerful?" Lightly, Kate licked the shell of Alexi's ear.

"Yes." Alexi's voice was rough and Kate could hear the arousal in that one word.

"I want to feel that." She pushed her hands under Alexi's T-shirt, then paused and waited for a sign of refusal from Alexi. When none came, she ran her hands up but stopped just short of touching her breasts. "Can you give that to me?"

Alexi arched her back and pressed her breasts into Kate's hands. "I want to." Alexi covered one of Kate's hands, but instead of pulling it away, she closed her fingers, squeezing Alexi's nipple. "I'll try."

"Good. Because I'm going to show you how incredible you made me feel."

Alexi trembled. Kate slowly undressed her and when Alexi tried to help, she gently removed her hands and resumed her task. Then Kate stood and lifted her own T-shirt over her head. She shoved aside any self-consciousness under the heat of Alexi's gaze as she bared herself completely. This time, she wanted no barriers between them.

When she returned to lie next to Alexi, they both sighed at the friction of skin on skin. Kate kissed Alexi's shoulder then littered a trail of them across her collarbone. She took her time, thoroughly exploring Alexi's body with her mouth and hands. When Alexi's hands wandered, Kate didn't stop them, not wanting her to feel restricted. Alexi's touch excited her, even while her patience was stretched to the limit. Kate trembled with the effort of holding herself back.

Kate stoked Alexi's arousal, letting her fingers drift high on Alexi's thigh but avoiding the final few inches that would carry her farther. She waited for a cue from Alexi, content to give back that small measure of control if it would comfort Alexi.

"Show me." Alexi's soft entreaty for more nearly undid Kate.

But she held back for a moment longer. Then, watching Alexi's face, she slid two fingers inside, just enough to feel Alexi's muscles trying to draw her deeper. Alexi was so wet, so ready, and Kate didn't see a hint of hesitation in her expression. When she eased in farther and out again, Alexi's eyes drifted closed and she moaned—a throaty sound that sent a shaft of pleasure through Kate. Her own body clamored for relief, enticing her with promises of ecstasy if she would indulge in just a few strokes.

"God, you feel good," Kate whispered.

Alexi gasped and wrapped her arms tight around Kate. As Kate led her higher, Alexi pressed her face into Kate's neck, kissing and sucking her.

"Can I tell you a secret?" Kate asked.

Alexi nodded against Kate's shoulder. Kate slid her fingers nearly all the way out and waited, then punctuated her next words with a steady thrust.

"I love the way you bite your lip when you fuck me."

Alexi cried out as her body jerked, then pulsed rhythmically against Kate's hand. Kate continued stroking, even after the first wave gave way to a second, and finally Alexi pulled her hand away.

"Thank you," Kate said against her temple.

Alexi laughed. "What you said…what you just did to me, and then you say thank you. I think that should be the other way around."

Kate smiled. "Well, then let's just say the feeling is mutual."

Chapter Nineteen

Kate wove her way through the crowd filling the tables all around her. She smiled when she spotted Alexi working behind the bar with a towel tucked into the waistband of her black slacks. She swung foam-capped mugs onto a tray, then grabbed a plate of onion rings from the window that led to the kitchen. Kate didn't even want to think about what perils awaited Alexi's white silk blouse if Kate didn't get her out of there soon. She slipped between groups of customers and rounded the bar.

After Alexi deposited a glass in front of a patron, Kate intercepted her before she could take another order.

"You hired bartenders. Just for tonight, let them handle it," she said resting a hand lightly in the small of Alexi's back. She pulled the towel free and dropped it under the bar.

"We had a rush. I came back here for only a minute."

Kate caught one of the bartenders smiling. "It looks like your whole night has been a rush. How long have you really been back here?"

"Five minutes."

"Don't lie to me or I'll make one of your employees tell me the truth."

"Half an hour, tops."

"Then I got here just in time." Kate squeezed Alexi's waist. "You have a good crowd for your grand reopening."

"Yes." Pride swelling in her heart, Alexi surveyed her business. In only six weeks, she had managed to rebuild In Left Field. She had opted not to decorate the interior exactly as it had been, instead giving it a fresh look for her brand-new start. She missed parts of her old décor, such as her father's basketball and the humidor.

But she had made an effort to add special touches when she redecorated. The three pool tables on one side of the room were restored antiques with leather pockets and thick, intricately carved legs. The entire bar had been wired with speakers that were attached to the largest of flat-panel televisions and could be turned on for special events. Many of her employees had returned, though a few who had already gotten jobs in the meantime had not.

"Let's go mingle with your guests." Kate began to ease her out from behind the bar.

"Okay, babe." Alexi touched Kate's arm to stall her. "But first, what can I get you to drink?"

"A Coke would be great."

"We're celebrating. Have some champagne or a beer."

"Just the soda, please."

"I keep telling you, I don't mind."

"And *I* keep telling *you*, I don't need to ingest any chemicals when I have you to make me feel good." Despite the increased amount of time Kate was spending in a bar lately, she actually hadn't had a drink in months. Alexi insisted that it didn't bother her for Kate to drink in front of her. But Kate continued to refuse, saying she'd never had more than the occasional beer with Paula and didn't miss it anyway.

"You're sweet. Are you sure?"

"Yes. You can stop asking me. Now, come on, I think I see some familiar faces over there."

Kate led Alexi through the crowd, stopping and waiting patiently when one well-wisher after another delayed Alexi. Finally, they reached a small group of people Alexi recognized as those closest to Kate. There was Kate's best friend, Paula, whom Alexi had come to know well since Kate had enlisted her as a manual laborer during the bar's restoration. An attractive woman stood next to Paula. Her expression was soft and her eyes sparkled when she looked at Paula. And her fingertips brushed Paula's sleeve when she spoke to her.

Kate's partner, Jason, wrapped an arm around her shoulders in greeting as she stepped into their circle. Alexi hung back for a moment, watching as Kate's friends greeted her. Alexi sensed Jason hadn't always been completely okay with Kate's decision to get involved with her. But in recent weeks he seemed to have come around. Perhaps the change had come as the time had passed since Alexi's case was closed.

Alexi hadn't been in touch with either Ron or Danielle, but she'd heard that Ron was standing by Danielle. He'd hired an attorney, but the notoriously slow justice system hadn't made any progress in prosecuting Danielle yet. Alexi expected she would hear from the assistant district attorney when the court date neared, but as far as she was concerned she had already received all the resolution possible. Oddly enough, she couldn't summon a need for vengeance when she thought about Danielle. All she felt was sadness at the loss of two friends she'd once held dear.

"Hey, come here." Kate slipped her hand inside Alexi's elbow and drew her close.

"Alexi, you did good here," Jason said, nodding at the room around them.

"Thank you. And thanks for coming," Alexi said. "Hello, Paula."

"Alexi, the place looks great. Allow me to introduce Dr. Celeste Fields."

"It's lovely to meet you. I've heard so much about you." Alexi grasped Celeste's hand.

Celeste glanced nervously at Paula.

"Don't worry. She speaks highly of you," Alexi assured her.

"Good." Celeste smiled. "It's nice to meet you, too. I was here once, before the fire, and enjoyed myself. You've definitely done the place justice in the remodel as well."

"Thank you."

Paula raised her bottle. "A toast. To Alexi. All your hard work is paying off."

Glasses and bottles clinked together.

Kate laced her fingers into Alexi's, her eyes inviting a private moment among the festivities. Alexi smiled at the woman who had come to mean so much in just the span of two months. Kate had coaxed Alexi's heart open so patiently, erasing Alexi's usual panic. Alexi trusted Kate with her future, with her happiness, and with her love.

"What should we toast to?" Kate asked as she lifted her glass in one hand and took Alexi's hand with the other.

"To new beginnings," Alexi answered without hesitation.

About the Author

Born and raised in upstate New York, Erin Dutton now lives and works in middle Tennessee. But she makes as many treks back north as she can squeeze into a year, because her beloved nephews and nieces grow faster every time she is away. In her free time she enjoys reading and playing golf.

Her previous novels include four romances: 2008 Golden Crown Literary Awards Finalist *Sequestered Hearts*, *Fully Involved*, *A Place to Rest*, and *Designed for Love*. She is also a contributor to *Erotic Interludes 5: Road Games* and *Romantic Interludes 1: Discovery* from Bold Strokes Books. Look for her upcoming title, *A Perfect Match*, in 2010.

Books Available From Bold Strokes Books

The High Priest and the Idol by Jane Fletcher. Jemeryl and Tevi's relationship is put to the test when the Guardian sends Jemeryl on a mission that puts her not only in harm's way, but back into the sights of a previous lover. (978-1-60282-085-2)

Point of Ignition by Erin Dutton. Amid a blaze that threatens to consume them both, firefighter Kate Chambers and property owner Alexi Clark redefine love and trust. (978-1-60282-084-5)

Secrets in the Stone by Radclyffe. Reclusive sculptor Rooke Tyler suddenly finds herself the object of two very different women's affections, and choosing between them will change her life forever. (978-1-60282-083-8)

Dark Garden by Jennifer Fulton. Vienna Blake and Mason Cavender are sworn enemies—who can't resist each other. Something has to give. (978-1-60282-036-4)

Late in the Season by Felice Picano. Set on Fire Island, this is the story of an unlikely pair of friends—a gay composer in his late thirties and an eighteen-year-old schoolgirl. (978-1-60282-082-1)

Punishment with Kisses by Diane Anderson-Minshall. Will Megan find the answers she seeks about her sister Ashley's murder or will her growing relationship with one of Ash's exes blind her to the real truth? (978-1-60282-081-4)

September Canvas by Gun Brooke. When Deanna Moore meets TV personality Faythe she is reluctantly attracted to her, but will Faythe side with the people spreading rumors about Deanna? (978-1-60282-080-7)

No Leavin' Love by Larkin Rose. Beautiful, successful Mercedes Miller thinks she can resume her affair with ranch foreman Sydney Campbell, but the rules have changed. (978-1-60282-079-1)

Between the Lines by Bobbi Marolt. When romance writer Gail Prescott meets actress Tannen Albright, she develops feelings that she usually only experiences through her characters. (978-1-60282-078-4)

Blue Skies by Ali Vali. Commander Berkley Levine leads an elite group of pilots on missions ordered by her ex-lover Captain Aidan Sullivan and everything is on the line—including love. (978-1-60282-077-7)

The Lure by Felice Picano. When Noel Cummings is recruited by the police to go undercover to find a killer, his life will never be the same. (978-1-60282-076-0)

Death of a Dying Man by J.M. Redmann. Mickey Knight, Private Eye and partner of Dr. Cordelia James, doesn't need a drop-dead gorgeous assistant—not until nature steps in. (978-1-60282-075-3)

Justice for All by Radclyffe. Dell Mitchell goes undercover to expose a human traffic ring and ends up in the middle of an even deadlier conspiracy. (978-1-60282-074-6)

Sanctuary by I. Beacham. Cate Canton faces one major obstacle to her goal of crushing her business rival, Dita Newton—her uncontrollable attraction to Dita. (978-1-60282-055-5)

The Sublime and Spirited Voyage of Original Sin by Colette Moody. Pirate Gayle Malvern finds the presence of an abducted seamstress, Celia Pierce, a welcome distraction until the captive comes to mean more to her than is wise. (978-1-60282-054-8)

Suspect Passions by VK Powell. Can two women, a city attorney and a beat cop, put aside their differences long enough to see that they're perfect for each other? (978-1-60282-053-1)

Just Business by Julie Cannon. Two women who come together—each for her own selfish needs—discover that love can never be as simple as a business transaction. (978-1-60282-052-4)

Sistine Heresy by Justine Saracen. Adrianna Borgia, survivor of the Borgia court, presents Michelangelo with the greatest temptations of his life while struggling with soul-threatening desires for the painter Raphaela. (978-1-60282-051-7)

Radical Encounters by Radclyffe. An out-of-bounds, outside-the-lines collection of provocative, superheated erotica by award-winning romance and erotica author Radclyffe. (978-1-60282-050-0)

Thief of Always by Kim Baldwin & Xenia Alexiou. Stealing a diamond to save the world should be easy for Elite Operative Mishael Taylor, but she didn't figure on love getting in the way. (978-1-60282-049-4)

X by JD Glass. When X-hacker Charlie Riven is framed for a crime she didn't commit, she accepts help from an unlikely source—sexy Treasury Agent Elaine Harper. (978-1-60282-048-7)

The Middle of Somewhere by Clifford Henderson. Eadie T. Pratt sets out on a road trip in search of a new life and ends up in the middle of somewhere she never expected. (978-1-60282-047-0)

Paybacks by Gabrielle Goldsby. Cameron Howard wants to avoid her old nemesis Mackenzie Brandt but their high school reunion brings up more than just memories. (978-1-60282-046-3)

Uncross My Heart by Andrews & Austin. When a radio talk show diva sets out to interview a female priest, the two women end up at odds and neither heaven nor earth is safe from their feelings. (978-1-60282-045-6)

Fireside by Cate Culpepper. Mac, a therapist, and Abby, a nurse, fall in love against the backdrop of friendship, healing, and defending one's own within the Fireside shelter. (978-1-60282-044-9)

A Pirate's Heart by Catherine Friend. When rare book librarian Emma Boyd searches for a long-lost treasure map, she learns the hard way that pirates still exist in today's world—some modern pirates steal maps, others steal hearts. (978-1-60282-040-1)

Trails Merge by Rachel Spangler. Parker Riley escapes the high-powered world of politics to Campbell Carson's ski resort—and their mutual attraction produces anything but smooth running. (978-1-60282-039-5)

Dreams of Bali by C.J. Harte. Madison Barnes worships work, power, and success, and she's never allowed anyone to interfere—that is, until she runs into Karlie Henderson Stockard. Aeros EBook (978-1-60282-070-8)

The Limits of Justice by John Morgan Wilson. Benjamin Justice and reporter Alexandra Templeton search for a killer in a mysterious compound in the remote California desert. (978-1-60282-060-9)

Designed for Love by Erin Dutton. Jillian Sealy and Wil Johnson don't much like each other, but they do have to work together—and what they desire most is not what either of them had planned. (978-1-60282-038-8)

Calling the Dead by Ali Vali. Six months after Hurricane Katrina, NOLA Detective Sept Savoie is a cop who thinks making a relationship work is harder than catching a serial killer—but her current case may prove her wrong. (978-1-60282-037-1)

Shots Fired by MJ Williamz. Kyla and Echo seem to have the perfect relationship and the perfect life until someone shoots at Kyla—and Echo is the most likely suspect. (978-1-60282-035-7)

truelesbianlove.com by Carsen Taite. Mackenzie Lewis and Dr. Jordan Wagner have very different ideas about love, but they discover that truelesbianlove is closer than a click away. Aeros EBook (978-1-60282-069-2)

Justice at Risk by John Morgan Wilson. Benjamin Justice's blind date leads to a rare opportunity for legitimate work, but a reckless risk changes his life forever. (978-1-60282-059-3)

Run to Me by Lisa Girolami. Burned by the four-letter word called love, the only thing Beth Standish wants to do is run for—or maybe from—her life. (978-1-60282-034-0)

Split the Aces by Jove Belle. In the neon glare of Sin City, two women ride a wave of passion that threatens to consume them in a world of fast money and fast times. (978-1-60282-033-3)

Uncharted Passage by Julie Cannon. Two women on a vacation that turns deadly face down one of nature's most ruthless killers—and find themselves falling in love. (978-1-60282-032-6)

Night Call by Radclyffe. All medevac helicopter pilot Jett McNally wants to do is fly and forget about the horror and heartbreak she left behind in the Middle East, but anesthesiologist Tristan Holmes has other plans. (978-1-60282-031-9)

Lake Effect Snow by C.P. Rowlands. News correspondent Annie T. Booker and FBI Agent Sarah Moore struggle to stay one step ahead of disaster as Annie's life becomes the war zone she once reported on. Aeros EBook (978-1-60282-068-5)

I Dare You by Larkin Rose. Stripper by night, corporate raider by day, Kelsey's only looking for sex and power, until she meets a woman who stirs her heart and her body. (978-1-60282-030-2)

Truth Behind the Mask by Lesley Davis. Erith Baylor is drawn to Sentinel Pagan Osborne's quiet strength, but the secrets between them strain duty and family ties. (978-1-60282-029-6)

Cooper's Deale by KI Thompson. Two would-be lovers and a decidedly inopportune murder spell trouble for Addy Cooper, no matter which way the cards fall. (978-1-60282-028-9)

Romantic Interludes 1: Discovery ed. by Radclyffe and Stacia Seaman. An anthology of sensual, erotic contemporary love stories from the best-selling Bold Strokes authors. (978-1-60282-027-2)

A Guarded Heart by Jennifer Fulton. The last place FBI Special Agent Pat Roussel expects to find herself is assigned to an illicit private security gig baby-sitting a celebrity. (Ebook) (978-1-60282-067-8)

Saving Grace by Jennifer Fulton. Champion swimmer Dawn Beaumont, injured in a car crash she caused, flees to Moon Island, where scientist Grace Ramsay welcomes her. (Ebook) (978-1-60282-066-1)

The Sacred Shore by Jennifer Fulton. Successful tech industry survivor Merris Randall does not believe in love at first sight until she meets Olivia Pearce. (Ebook) (978-1-60282-065-4)

Passion Bay by Jennifer Fulton. Two women from different ends of the earth meet in paradise. Author's expanded edition. (Ebook) (978-1-60282-064-7)

Never Wake by Gabrielle Goldsby. After a brutal attack, Emma Webster becomes a self-sentenced prisoner inside her condo—until the world outside her window goes silent. (Ebook) (978-1-60282-063-0)

The Caretaker's Daughter by Gabrielle Goldsby. Against the backdrop of a nineteenth-century English country estate, two women struggle to find love. (Ebook) (978-1-60282-062-3)

Simple Justice by John Morgan Wilson. When a pretty-boy cokehead is murdered, former LA reporter Benjamin Justice and his reluctant new partner, Alexandra Templeton, must unveil the real killer. (978-1-60282-057-9)

Remember Tomorrow by Gabrielle Goldsby. Cees Bannigan and Arieanna Simon find that a successful relationship rests in remembering the mistakes of the past. (978-1-60282-026-5)

Put Away Wet by Susan Smith. Jocelyn "Joey" Fellows has just been savagely dumped—when she posts an online personal ad, she discovers more than just the great sex she expected. (978-1-60282-025-8)

Homecoming by Nell Stark. Sarah Storm loses everything that matters—family, future dreams, and love—will her new "straight" roommate cause Sarah to take a chance at happiness? (978-1-60282-024-1)

Falling Star by Gill McKnight. Solley Rayner hopes a few weeks with her family will help heal her shattered dreams, but she hasn't counted on meeting a woman who stirs her heart. (978-1-60282-023-4)

Lethal Affairs by Kim Baldwin and Xenia Alexiou. Elite operative Domino is no stranger to peril, but her investigation of journalist Hayley Ward will test more than her skills. (978-1-60282-022-7)

A Place to Rest by Erin Dutton. Sawyer Drake doesn't know what she wants from life until she meets Jori Diamantina—only trouble is, Jori doesn't seem to share her desire. (978-1-60282-021-0)

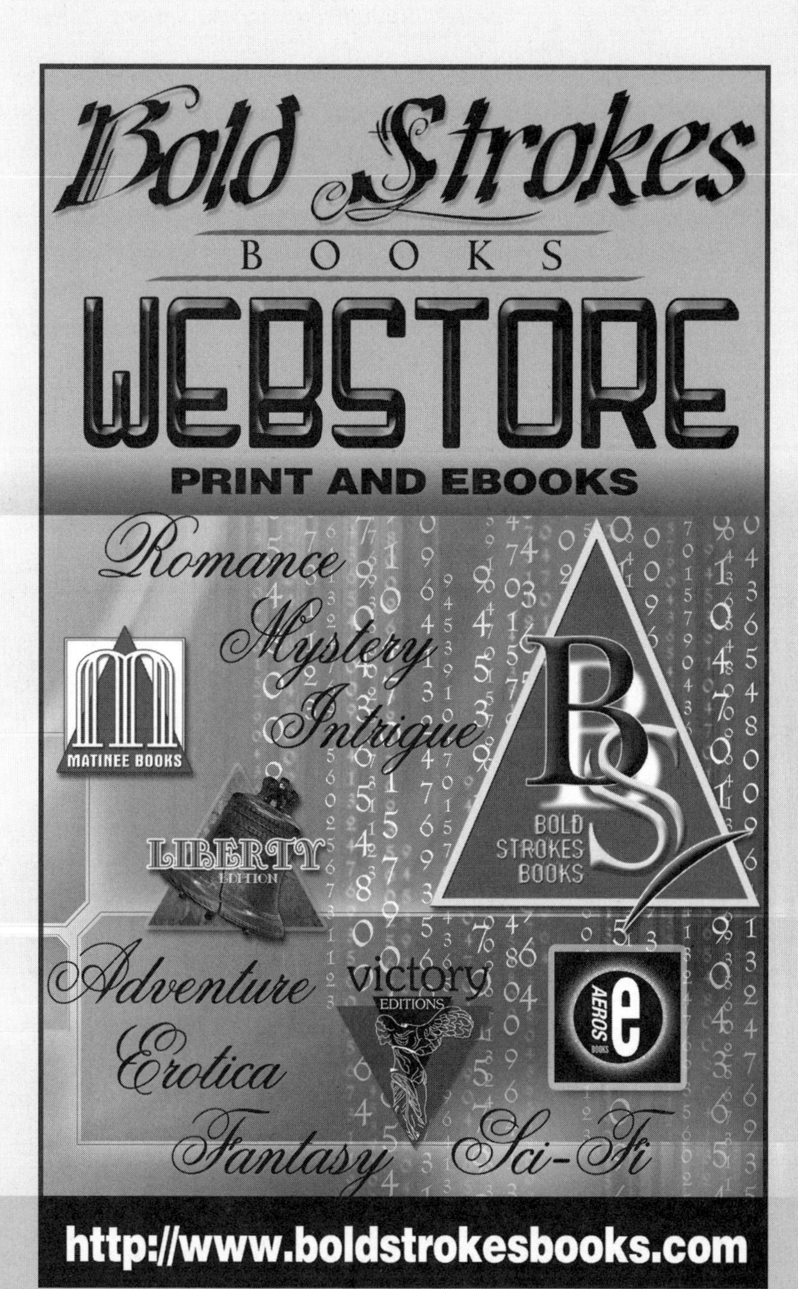
Bold Strokes
BOOKS
WEBSTORE
PRINT AND EBOOKS
Romance
Mystery
Intrigue
MATINEE BOOKS
LIBERTY
EDITION
BOLD
STROKES
BOOKS
Adventure
victory
EDITIONS
AEROS
e
BOOKS
Erotica
Fantasy
Sci-Fi
http://www.boldstrokesbooks.com